FROM LIKES
TO LATE
NIGHTS

By Lala B.

Contents

Trigger Warnings

Baby I am going to hold your hand while we read these trigger warnings together. If any of them make you feel any type of way just close the book, I will not feel bad. Now if you're still here let's get to the good stuff.

- Fuckin and lots of it.
- Foul language
- Child abuse mentioned
- Obsessive behavior
- Stalking
- Violent scenes

Synopsis

Dr. Arlani James didn't plan on falling—especially not for a man she met through a DM. Between running her clinic and co-parenting like a boss with her ex, she thought her love life was on pause. But when her ex's jealous new girlfriend shows up as her patient, throwing shade and stirring drama, Arlani finds herself craving an escape. Enter Kairo Levi—dark chocolate skin, locs pulled back, body built like a prayer—and all it took was one heart emoji to make her start blushing through her scrubs. Late-night chats turn into workout FaceTime fantasies, and soon Arlani is tangled in a romance hotter than anything she's written in her journals. But passion comes with a price, and not everyone's happy about her relationship glow-up. Now she's caught between her peace, her past, a jealous girlfriend and the kind of love that could expose her deepest desires. Some messages you delete. Others... you surrender to.

Chapter One

Dr. Arlani James

"Bestieeee." Mymy, who is my best friend and pretty much my sister from another mother sing songs as she walks in my front door carrying a plate of food that smells so delicious per usual. She's on veggies and dessert duty tonight while I have the meat which I went with honey glazed lamb chops then the side homemade mashed potatoes.

"You smelling good coming in here. What did you decide on?" I ask the moment she gets in the kitchen and sits the serving dishes on the island.

"Just some asparagus sautéed in garlic butter and one of our classic favorites— chocolate chip cookies." She answers and my stomach growls from all the food smells in here. Since buying our townhouses right next to each other after deciding to make the move from Miami to Birmingham, Alabama we alternate who cooks dinner for the week. It's usually me, her, and my son Zion but it's Darren his dad week with him even though he is around often anyway. Darren and I started out as friends and remained that way for years but one night out drinking turned into a nine-month weird trial period to see if we could actually be a couple for the sake of our growing baby. For me it was a heavy no, I sometimes think that Darren felt different but where he lacked in a relationship for me he made up tenfold as a father to Zion. That man was there for every appointment, took parenting classes with me, and actually participated. Then on top of all that when I said I wanted to move he found a job then bought a house for them about thirty minutes away. He even paid to have my place packed up and transported here.

"So, I have a date this weekend with that guy Chance we met at the restaurant last week." I informed her and watched as her face morphed into this huge clown smile that made me almost spit out the mashed potatoes in my mouth from laughing so hard at her.

"Well it's about time you put yourself out there woman. Between you working to become a doctor and then having Zion you haven't had much of a social life that involved the opposite sex, well besides ya slip up wit Darren of course." She so dramatically describes my nonexistent love life for the past nine almost ten years while pointing her fork left and right.

"Look heffa I know I haven't had much of a love life but my parents sacrificed everything so I could get through medical school with the least amount of debt possible, you know that. So, I am enjoying myself now and besides he was just too damn sexy to pass up." We tapped wine glasses on that note then continued with our meal.

"Hey, whatever happened to the personal trainer hotty?" She asks as we're putting the dishes in the dishwasher and wiping down the counters.

"That was just a social media flirt girl, plus he lives in Montgomery and I'm sure his fine ass has a woman or at least a few that think they're his woman. I don't need that type of drama. I have taken his classes a few times to keep all these curves looking good though." I reply while envisioning his dark chocolate muscles flexing as we worked out in my one-on-one classes. I told myself I can't have him in real life, but the classes I take will suffice.

"You may be right, but I'd still go for him if he shows interest. I mean the man is fine as hell, in shape, no kids, own his business, and home. I just don't want you putting all your eggs in one basket friend after just getting out there." She expresses.

"I hear you but something about that man scares me like his dick would fuck my whole world up. I've seen that print during our workouts no matter how hard he tries to hide it and lawd I've dreamt about him wrapping those big ass hands around my neck while. You know what let me get ready for bed." I fix myself while she's laughing at me then gives me a kiss on the cheek and heads for the door. I'm sure she has one of her late-night rendezvous on schedule anyway. Sometimes I wish I could be like her just free spirited with my sexual life but I crave a deeper connection or a lot of alcohol for my pussy to work and seeing as a sister isn't getting drunk around anyone my only option is getting that deeper connection. After getting my hygiene in order I lay in my bed scrolling through Tic looking at random videos until I land on one of *his* most recent videos and shit if that man doesn't look edible with his tatted chest and arms all out dripping with sweat as he does these damn side to side pull ups with his long neat dreads pulled back in a ponytail. I like the video and leave the muscle arm emoji and just as I am about to close out the app I get a notification about a message.

TrainerKai: Hi beautiful I didn't see you on my schedule this week.

HeavenlyLani: I've had a busy week. I did still work out though. I got some yoga in this morning before my shift at the clinic.

TrainerKai: That's good but you make my week better when I get to see that pretty face of yours. Speaking of seeing your face I have a charity event for the Charleston youth center at the gym in a couple weeks and would love for you to come through.

HeavenlyLani: I'm always down to support the kids send me the info and I will make sure I can fit it in my schedule.

TrainerKai: Check your email beautiful and it's cool if you bring a plus one. Now get some sleep I'm sure you have an early morning at the clinic. 😉

HeavenlyLani: I got it and good night to you too.

I had to fan myself after messaging that man but he was right I do have an early morning at my family clinic called The Blooming Center for Holistic Wellness. I like to blend modern medicine with natural ways of healing to keep our bodies in tip top shape. I'm the ob/gyn of the clinic then I have three other doctors two of which went to school with me and were ready for a change in pace then there's the third doctor who is a local. It was a bit of a challenge convincing them that the community would be accepting of three black women and a black man opening a clinic in a majority red state, but we have been open for five years now with steady patients. I can contribute that to us doing local pop-up shops before we opened and regularly having our own health event doing free testing as well as check-ups to those without insurance. Business is picking up so we are looking to add two new doctors to the roster but there has been some talks about having to hire at least one white person before rumors start about us possibly being racist or some shit but I just want this to be a place for us to feel safe with those that look like us so they can kiss my whole ass on that note. Before I know it's time to get ready for work and it is Tuesday, so my patient list is full including two new patients. Pulling up to my clinic always brings a smile to my face even on tough days.

"Good morning, Ms. James you are booked up today with regulars and two new patients. I left the patient files on your desk along with a pick me up." Cherish my assistant, who sometimes works the front desk when all the nurses or receptionist are busy, fills me in on my day.

"What would I do without you Cherish, thanks." I thank her then walk back to my office. My first few patients were my regulars, the one I'm walking to the front desk is Mrs. Truman one of my more trying patients to say the least.

"OK now Mrs. Truman I will schedule for one of our nurses to come by this week and make sure you are keeping up with you medicine as well as the natural regimen I put you on." I explain to her again after handing the file over to the medical assistant that came in earlier. We have a couple nurses that make home visits to some of our elderly patients who either don't have much family or none at all.

"You are such an angel Dr. James thank you baby." She gives me a hug as she usually does then walks out to board the transportation van we also offer free of charge to the patients since most of their insurance covers the rides anyway.

"Ok Tracy I am stepping out for my lunch. I will be back in an hour." I announce then walk back to my office to grab my keys and purse then I head out the back exit. Before I can even get in my car Mymy is calling me.

"Yes chick I'm on my way to the spot now." I cut her off before she even starts her normal rant about me being late. We found this soul food restaurant about a month ago and decided we would try everything on the menu at least once. Today I am trying their smothered pork chops, and I know as a health professional I should be staying away from foods like this but I am a believer that everything in moderation is okay. Thankfully the place isn't packed yet and I snag a parking spot right next to Mymy's new white Audi truck. I am so proud of her opening her own interior decorating boutique called MoodHaus in downtown and when I say they have been after my girl like white on rice honey. Everyone wants her African modern chic style she has going on in her boutique, I even have a few of her furniture pieces along with art throughout my place. After checking my lipstick and touching up my makeup I hop out my white Lexus then head inside the restaurant to find Mymy flirting with some fine ass redbone with all this thick ass hair pulled back in a low ponytail. He's a little slim for my taste but my girl does not discriminate, and I don't blame her one bit but I will be happy when she finds someone to settle down with.

"Umhmm." I clear my throat walking up behind the guy since he is blocking her view of me and my seat.

"Ooooh hi bestie this is Prince, and he was just leaving." She introduces us. He turns to shake my hand then he looks back over his shoulder to wink at Mymy with a sly grin on his face. She acts bashful putting her head down cheeks with a light hue of red and pulls a strand of her passion twist with seashells hanging from it behind her ear. He leaves the restaurant after going to the counter to grab his food and I take my seat.

"OK ma'am was that the hotty you had the late-night cap with?" I question her sitting my purse in the seat next to us.

"No, I just met him. He thinks he big shit cause he owns that clothing store two doors down from my shop. He has been trying to get at me for weeks, something about his ass is rubbing me the wrong way though." She answers and that is my girl she may be free spirited having sex with who she wants when she wants but that girl always pays attention to her intuition about people.

"You have your taser?" I ask her as the waiter comes over with our food and damn this food smells amazing. Every dish we have tried here thus far has been amazing. The owner and his wife are patients of mine at the clinic. Mymy pats her purse to answer me since she has decided to straight dig into her food. We eat and chat a bit more before we both have to head back to work. While driving back to the office I get a phone call from Chance.

"Hello beautiful, how is your day going?" He greets me as soon as I answer and I have to admit it makes me blush a bit. When I woke up this morning, I had a text message from him as well wishing me a great day.

"I am doing great just left lunch with my best friend that was with me the night we met. How is your day going?" I reply.

"My day is going well. I made sixty thousand in commissions selling one of the cheaper listings just now. I can't wait for our dinner this weekend though. Well, I am being summoned. I will give you a call later." He says then ends the call once I say bye. That fool just received one strike, I can't stand a man that brags about his money. I am hoping this is not a mistake, but he has two more before I cut his ass off, well that depends on what strike two is. I exit my car once I park in my spot behind the clinic and enter my office. Once I get settled at my desk my assistant comes through on the phone intercom to let me know my next patient is waiting in room six. I gather up my stethoscope and the patient's folder which I haven't had a chance to look over just yet but the moment I walk in the room I wish I would have read it sooner to prepare myself to be face to face with Darren's girlfriend Farah. I have never met her in person, but he has showed me pictures after Zion let it slipped that he heard him on the phone with her a few times. She apparently has been asking him why he hasn't introduced her to his son seeing as they have been dating for over six months now. I'm just hoping he hasn't made it seem like it's all me.

"Good afternoon Ms. Peterson, I'm Dr. James. I see you're in for a pap smear as well as STD screening and the nurse has already come in to draw your blood." I get right to the point because I can see the look on her face and the weird energy rolling off her.

"Oh," Farah says, tilting her head, "I didn't expect you to be the doctor." She scrunches up her face for a second but quickly fixes her expression but not quick enough.

"Well, I own the clinic and don't worry I treat all my patients the same no matter who they are dating. Now are there any concerns you have that you want to go over?" I ask her as professionally as I can while calling over the intercom for one of my nurses to come in as I always do. She looks over at me with concern in her eyes after sensing the tension in the room while I setup what I need to perform the test. Farah catches on that I am not going to feed into her attitude and shakes her head no. The nurse hands her a hospital gown and instructs her to change into it in the attached bathroom. Once she comes out I have her get into position on the bed and perform the pap smear then take another for the BV test she clearly needs from the yellowish discharge she has leaking from her vagina.

"Ok I took a swab for your pap smear as well as to test for BV as you have a discharge with a yellowish tint and mild odor. We have our own fully equipped lab upstairs so you will be notified in forty-eight to seventy-two hours from today in our patient portal. Do you have any questions?" I gave her the run-down pf everything that was to come next like I normally do then wait for her to say something and of course she does the moment my nurse leaves to take the swabs to the lab for testing.

"You must think you are something special because you're a doctor don't you. Well, you're not. You're clearly just another bitter baby mama who's not over her ex." Her weak ass attempt at reading me only makes me laugh.

"Lil girl let me tell your insecure ass something I am something special and not just because I went to med school, did my residence at Johns Hopkins, then moved here opened my own clinic, purchased my own home, all while being a damn good mother to my child but because I am confident and respect myself enough not to be jealous of any woman." I emphasize that last part for her insecure ass because that is the only reason she could think I am bitter about a damn thing.

"If you're so confident and respect yourself then why the hell are you being such a bitch about Darren introducing me to his son? We are trying to build a family of our own." This bitch is seriously testing my patience.

"I think you need to have a conversation with your man because it's not me holding him back. All he has to do is let me know when he's serious about someone." I inform her making sure to add in that last part because that is what we agreed to and grin the moment my comment registers in her small brain.

"Whatever I will definitely have a talk with him, and you better not tell him about my test results either." She hops off the exam table then leaves the room to get dressed and I leave to go to my next patient before that cottage cheese pussy ass bitch have me acting in my place of business. The rest of my patients are a breeze even the other new patient who turned out to be a young girl looking for the best birth control options since she recently turned eighteen and has decided she's ready. I gave her some options and had a bit of a girls talk with her since she told me she just aged out the foster system. I also gave her Mymy's card to go in about a job to keep her mind from worrying about sex and put some money in her pockets instead. When I texted Mymy about it, she was happy I sent her to her, that's one of the things I love about Mymy well Myasia she is the most caring person I know. I finish gathering my things and head to grab me some takeout since Mymy just let me know she was going to be late with a client and wouldn't be able to do dinner tonight.

Chapter Two

Kairo Levi

Damn she is just perfection wrapped in brown skin. My daily routine has changed to include staring at her damn photos the moment I wake up fully then start moving around but soon I will be able to roll over to see her angelic face in person.

"So, you're still stalking the poor woman, I thought you were going to invite her to the charity event?" My little brother Nasir says walking into my office in the back of my gym.

"Shut up you little twit, I did invite her, but did you get what I requested it?" I don't even bother looking up at him because I know he has that annoying know it all grin he usually has when he thinks he's caught me.

"Yes, oh mighty Kairo." He says sarcastically bending over at the waist like he's bowing to a king then lays a manila envelope on my desk that I quickly snatch up and pull out the contents.

"What's so special about this one? I mean she is beautiful, extremely intelligent, and has wealth don't get me wrong but you've always been the fuck em and move on type. You seemed obsessed, should I be worried?" He questions me taking off his suit jacket then taking a seat on the black velvet sofa to the right of my desk. I still don't bother to look up at him I just neatly lay the papers on my desk and start scanning over them.

        "I can't tell exactly what it is but no little brother you don't need to worry and thank you for this." I point to the papers, and he simply nods his head then grabs the remote to turn the tv on to watch the cameras in the gym then he switches to his tech office. I continue to look over the papers memorizing every piece of information how my pops taught me. Nasir and I grew up simple with our moms Akilah and our father Omari. Dad was a professor of mathematics and Mom was a nurse but has since retired along with dad and are living the good life. Growing up our childhood was happy, normal family drama occasionally, we took family trips where we always learned something about where we were because that was one nonnegotiable for my parents. Education and specifically pattern recognition when it came to Pops. I caught on to all the things my three siblings and I thought were weird back then but now use in our business day to day to make sure people are not trying to get over on us mentally or financially. Being the second oldest child, but the oldest boy came with the unspoken responsibility to watch over my siblings so I've always been an overachiever to make sure if anything happened, they could always lean on me. Something in my angels file catches my eye about her little boy Zion and I hope it won't be a problem when we become a family.

"Kai, are you going somewhere nigga?" My brother questioned the moment he notices my go bag sitting next to my desk on the floor.

"Yes, I'll be back tomorrow night." Is all I give him because seriously how do I explain what I'm about to do without him calling our parents and possibly having me committed even if his punk ass isn't wrapped too tight either. He spends another hour watching sports recap then heads out. I grab my criss cross shredder to bring it close to me and drop each document in one by one. Pops made sure all of us were tech savvy, but Nasir took it to another level with his tech company, it's nothing that man can't find out about someone with his hacking skills. I remember the high school football team thought they were going to bully him, and he released every last one of their positive STD test results in the school chat room. It was an uproar for weeks after that with the girlfriends trying to figure out who each of them got it from. Once I check to make sure everything in the gym is locked down tight, I hop in my black-on-black Benz and head to my destination that's only about an hour and a half away from me. I check my approximate arrival time, and it has me around one a.m. which is perfect, my angel will be fast asleep by then. I spend the whole hour and a half watching her new videos of her in the clinic, hanging out with her best friend, and some old videos. I like that my girl is smart, she doesn't post her pictures or videos while she's at a location she does it later. The only person that needs to be tracking her movements is me and checking the link to her phone my brother sent over she hasn't picked up for a couple of hours. I notice her best friend's car isn't home, so I park right next to her white Benz and just smile at the fact we have the same car. I get out heading up the short steps to her porch then let myself in using the key I had made and quickly set the alarm which I am going to have a conversation with her about changing that later. I make my way upstairs since she already has two cameras downstairs then a third at the door and I have already tapped into those. I quietly enter her large master bedroom and instantly feel at home in her African inspired décor. Her walls are a neutral light tan color, but every painting has vibrant shades of green, orange, yellow, black, and brown. Her bed is this huge four poster medium tan with sheer curtains all around tied to each post. I walk around to where she's sleeping on her side, hair wrapped up in a scarf, mouth partially opened as she lightly snores, and I swear those juicy heart shaped lips of hers make me want to lay a kiss on them right now but I'm sure that would be a little awkward right now. She chose a nice dark green comforter with crisp white silk sheets to play off the green in the artwork. I shake my head to get myself out the trance she has me in admiring her sleeping beauty and get to work placing a small wireless camera in one of her many plants in her room this one facing the bed. I placed another in the massive walk-in closet then went down the hall to place one in her home library, which I notice my girl likes all types of books but mainly freaky as hell. Once I'm done I head downstairs, but I hear the door unlocking so I hide over in her home office. I hear giggling from a woman after the door closes and kissing.

"Damn I can't wait to get in this pussy baby." Some big ass nigga groans while feeling up on who I now recognize to be Myasia, my angels best friend. We need to have a talk about her best friend bringing random broke ass niggas to her home in the middle of the night.

"Whoa." She says when she bumps into the living room sofa, and I notice the confused look on her face from where I'm standing in the doorway of the office. Since they haven't tried turning any lights on yet.

"You ok Mymy?" The dude questions.

"Yea I'm fine but I think my drunk ass has mistaken my bestie's house again. Yup we're definitely in her house." She starts to move but he stops her.

"Think your bestie would like to join us?" When that punk ass nigga finished his thought I almost stepped out the office but Mymy slapping the taste out that niggas mouth stopped me. I hear movement coming from upstairs, so I step fully into the office just in time for my angel to turn the light on and miss my movement.

"What the hell is going on down here?" She questions standing at the top of the steps wrapped in a black silk robe and rubbing her eyes. I can see her beautiful ass in the mirror since I left the door to the office open and it hangs on the wall right across from the door.

"Lani I'm so sorry."

"Mymy again bitch come on and who the hell is this nigga? You know what I don't even care just get out it's one in the damn morning and Mymy you need to get your shit together." She shouts and I like the fact that my girl has a backbone. Mymy looks so ashamed as she should and pulls the dude out the door in a hurry, but I notice how he's looking at my woman. She goes back upstairs once she sets the alarm, and I decide to leave another camera in her office to see my baby work. Once I think she's back in bed I head to check the camera's outside to make sure Mymy's trifling ass went into her house this time then head home.

Chapter Three

Arlani James

Today is my date with Chance and I am kind of nervous about it all of a sudden. We have been talking through text and the occasional video call but I'm not sure if I'm being too picky or what. Let's just say the nigga has some red flags but minor ones. Mymy is in my closet trying to help me find something to wear, she's been on her best behavior since her fuck up. I am still annoyed with her because she knows how I am about my personal space and other people energy hell she's just as bad so I don't get what was up with her the other night. We finally decide on some black ripped jeans, champagne colored long sleeve silk off the shoulder blouse, and some black wedges. I love this shirt because it hides my slightly big arms but thanks to Kai's work they have tightened up quite a bit. I throw on some rose gold accessories and put my mid back length knotless plaits in cute top bun.

"So is he picking you up babe?" She asked while sitting at the edge my bed while I spray myself with my favorite perfume that's a vanilla scent with hints of coconut and something else I never quite put my finger on but it's some type of citrus.

"Now you should know better. I am meeting him at the restaurant. He had me choose so I went with Sole, you know I love that place. It's such a vibe that even if things go bad he won't ruin it." She nods her head in agreement, and I check my phone for the time but get distracted by a message from Kai that brings a smile to my face.

"Dang he has you blushing before your date that's a good sign." She comments thinking it's Chance I am texting back, and I quickly correct her that it's Kai sending me this funny video. We graduated to texting each other last night because we kept missing each other online.

"So, about this chick Farah, you know I looked her ass up right." I just shake my head at her because I know the moment I got off the phone with her yesterday she was going to do that.

"Look Mymy don't go doing too much. I'm sure it will work itself out because I definitely don't want Darren's ass." I advise her.

"I hear you but something not right about that broad. Just watch her ass when she's around." I nod my head in response then take one more look at myself in my full-length black chrome framed mirror, grab my purse, and we both head out. I send a text message to Zion to say good night then get on the road. Pulling up to the restaurant I hand the valet my keys and spot Chance waiting by the door.

"Well damn you look gorgeous." He greets me kissing the top of my hand then spins me around to get a look at my ass and I'm cool with that at this point in my life. I used to be so self-conscious of my big butt and wide hips, but I've come to love every curve. Once we enter the restaurant, I can feel eyes on me as we wait for the hostess to seat us at the table he reserved but I brush it off as the normal men wandering eyes and sometimes women cause let's face it ya girl looks damn good.

"Here you go beautiful." Chances nods as he pulls out my chair for me then pushes my seat in. It's cute and I see he's trying to win some brownie points which he has a few but I'm still watching him.

"I am Jessica, and I will be your waitress for tonight. If you like we can start with your drink orders." The waitress introduces herself once he sits and we get comfortable. I notice he looks at her a little weird before looking back down at the drink menu and now I'm wondering what's that all about when she shifts her stance with a slight uncomfortable look.

"I will have a glass of La'mour white wine." I provide her with my order as he is still looking over the menu.

"Give me an old fashion made from your top shelf whiskey." He finally orders and his choice of drink reminds me of Darren when we all use to go out to dinner. He always chose a whiskey drink, I think he's tried every brand there is at this point. I am starting to think that I am tripping though because I swear someone is still watching me, but I can't figure out who it may be.

"Arlani... Hey is everything ok?" Chance reaches across the table and gently caresses my hand causing me to realize I had wandered into my head.

"Hmm oh I'm sorry about that everything is fine. Were you saying something?" I ask blinking a few times to bring myself back.

"Just asked how was your day at the clinic." He repeated the question I missed before.

"Oh the clinic was slow today, which it usually is on Friday's hence why we close early. How was your day at your brokerage firm?" Before he can answer the waitress has come with our drink orders and I take a much-needed sip of my wine to ease my nerves.

"Would like to order now?" I recognize she still has an uneasy energy with him and he has this weird look in his eye when he looks at her. We give her our orders and she rushes away.

"He do you know her or something?" I question him because at this point the behavior is getting way past weird.

"No I don't think so but there's no need to be jealous, I'm here with you and today was busy I closed one of my biggest commercial deals to date." He replies and I just look at this fool as if he's grown another head because who the hell said I would be jealous of any damn body. I chose to ignore his comment and actually begin to tune his ass out as all he is doing is going on and on about all the deals he closed this week along with how much he made. When a new waitress comes back with our food I know something is really up with the two of them now but I don't care to find out since this will be the last time I see this arrogant prick. I dig into my salmon and can't help but to moan with the lemon buttery flavors hit my taste buds.

"Dang I knew you thicker women loved your food but damn." He groans feening with annoyance and I am about to rip him a new one when the scent of bourbon, sandalwood, and vanilla hits my nose then I look up at the beautiful specimen of a man that it's attached to.

"I had a feeling that was you Lani." Even the way this man says my damn name makes my body heat up and seeing him in our one on one video workouts does not do him justice.

"Kai what are you doing way over here?" I stand to give him a church hug but he pulls me in close and I can't help but to close my eyes as I inhale his scent committing it to my memory.

"Umhm." Chance clears his throat. Kairo has me in such a trance I completely forget his pathetic ass is sitting there.

"Kairo Chance. Chance Kairo." I introduce them while still standing close to Kai who has his left hand still resting on my hip. Chance gets up from his seat I guess feeling intimidated by Kai's tall large frame standing over his slender but medium height build. Chance holds out is hand for Kai to shake and he does with a really firm grip.

"How do you two know each other?" Chance grimaces after snatching his hand from Kai's grip and it takes everything in me not to laugh.

"I'm the one who helps her keep this beautiful body of her's in shape not that she needs much help, don't you think so?" Kai responds for me inciting the heat in my cheeks to raise to a ten and I'm sure they are visibly red now. By what he just said though I wonder if he heard his comment about my eating before.

"No I guess not but if you don't mind, we are in the middle of a date." Chance states as he's reaching for my hand to sit but I place it on my hip and tilt my head because this fool can't be serious after the underhanded comments as well as the weird energy with the waitress who I have yet to see again.

"Well I was just here having some drinks with my brother and cousin, if you want, I will leave you two to it then." Kai looks down at me turning my head up and towards him by my chin to look me in the eyes as he waits for me to answer.

"No you are fine Kai I was just leaving, this so call date was over before you even stepped to the table." I reply finally. I feel like I could stare into his brown eyes for an eternity and he realizes his effect on me then has the nerve to put the cutest grin on his face. I can tell now he is going to be trouble for me if I'm not careful.

"Are you serious right now after I let you pick this bougie and expensive ass restaurant you think you're just going to walk up out of here with me getting nothing out of this?" Chance whisper yells as he hops from his seat trying to jump in my face but Kai has me moved behind him before he can get even a step closer to me.

"You can't afford the dinner that's cool lil nigga I gotcha but if you want those hands attached to your body I would advise you not to reach for her again, understood." Kai insults and warns him all in one breath. I am so incredibly turned on by Kai right now and this alpha male energy that's rolling off him in waves like a damn pheromone. I usually don't even like the alpha male type but something about him is rubbing me in all the right places.

"You know what you can have the fat bit-" Kai lays him out with one right hook before he can even finish his sentence.

"Hey I am going to have to ask you all to leave. You're disturbing our guest." A man I assume is the manager whispers while stretching his arm out towards the door. I grab my clutch and I see Kai gesture at two men just as large as him that are standing near the bar watching then they move towards the exit. Kai reaches for my hand and I place it in his as we walk towards the exit. Behind me I hear the manager trying to wake up a knocked out Chance and I giggle.

"We will be at the car bro." One of the guys I guess is his brother since they favor the most.

"You ok Lani?" He asks looking me in the eyes and caressing my cheek with his knuckles. If I didn't know any better I would say this man truly cares about me but he can't, can he. I mean this is our first time even meeting in person and I was just on a date with another man. He rubs his thumb against my cheek bringing me out of my running thoughts.

"Yea... yea I'm ok. Thanks for that back there I can't believe I agreed to go on a date with idiot." I sigh as I shake my head and turn to look away but he keeps me looking at him by my chin again.

"It was a mistake, it happens to the best of us. Now I know you're a smart woman so did you valet or park yourself?" Kai is seriously dishing out the compliments tonight and I'm not complaining one bit.

"Valet of course." I answer and he holds his hand out I assume for my ticket so I hand it to him then he walks over to the valet then he comes back to me as the guy leaves to get my car.

"So I am glad I got to see you outside of our workout videos before the charity event next week. At least I can somewhat prepare myself for how gorgeous you will look." This man must want me to go in this bathroom and hand him my soaked panties for him to take home the way he keeps talking to me. It's bad enough he has that deep smooth Luther voice.

"Well glad to know I'm not the only one who will be regulating their hormones." I shoot back as the valet pulls up with my car. Kai walks me to my door, opens it and helps me inside like the queen I am.

"Let me know when you make it home." I get the nerve to do something so I roll down my window once he closes my door and his tall ass has to squat down to rest his arms on my windowsill. I lean forward connecting my lips with his and try to pull back but he quickly kisses me back then places his hand firmly on my chin. He gives me two more quick kisses then leans his forehead against mine.

"You just made my night Lani. Now get home safe my angel." He professes then the look on his face changes to amused and I follow his line of sight to a groaning Chance being escorted out the restaurant rubbing his jaw. I can't help but laugh this time and that makes him spot me but he looks scared then I remember Kai is still standing next to my car plus what he told him before knocking his ass out.

"Don't do anything to get yourself in trouble please." I urged then batted my lashes at him seductively and he laughs lightly.

"Give me another kiss and boy scout promise I'll behave." I happily pull him in for another kiss but this one feels so much more heated then the last and I can't hold back the low moan I release.

"You better go before we do something you're not ready for baby." He urges me this time after releasing my chin then stands to his full six-foot three height and steps back. I practically come eye to eye with his huge bulge and I know I am going to be fantasizing about that shit all damn night.

"Ok but remember what you promised." I remind him and he leans down drawing a cross over his heart with his right hand up with a sexy ass grin on his face then taps the top of my car. I drive off biting my bottom lip already thinking about how it would feel to have him stretch me out.

Chapter Four

Kairo Levi

"So big bro did you get what you needed tonight?" Nasir questions me the moment I walk up to the car as they lean against the hood. When I told them I heard through the cameras that she was going on a damn date tonight they both jumped at the opportunity to have my back in busting up her date but clearly the lil fuck boy did that all on his own.

"Sure did. She's mine." I declare. Besides breaking up her date I did want to see if she was into me as much as I am into her and her initiating our first kiss sealed that for me.

"So, 0what are we doing about Mr. handsy?" Kareem my cousin ask next.

"I made a promise to my woman that I would behave myself tonight, so as long as he stays away I will too." I reply. I purposely kept her long enough to see him come out the restaurant then leave to make sure his bitch ass didn't try anything. Nasir looked him up while we were sipping our drinks and that nigga is a broke, lying, don't understand the word no bitch ass nigga. That little brokerage firm he owns is going under water, all the nigga credit cards are maxed out, and I'm sure his car will be reposed by the end of the month, hopefully by my tow company so I can personally see the look on his face. Kareem hops in his big boy GMC pick up truck and peels off then we do the same but I have Nasir drive since my angel has texted that she's made it home. We text back and forth for a bit before she lets me know she's going to get some sleep. I decide to watch her sleep for a bit since it's about ten minutes before we reach home and fuck I am glad I did.

"Mmhmm just like that Kai." She moans unbeknownst to my watching eyes and I am glad I have my headphone's in. She has her legs spread wide while bent at the knees and her rose on her clit. I can't wait to suck on that fat ass pussy of hers and I damn near lose it when she squirts all over her hand along with the towel I now notice up under her.

"Damn bro what are you watching so intently?" Nasir asks as he pulls into my garage and turns the car off.

"Nothing nigga I'll talk to you later." I bump fist with him as he shakes he head laughing at me while getting out the car.

"Fuck that wasn't enough. What has this man done to me?" I hear her question herself then turns the rose off and places it on her nightstand. When she reaches for then pulls out this dildo that looks like it has a suction cup on the end and gets out of bed sticking it to the wall I can't help but pull out my dick to let one off.

"Baby you're going to need something bigger than that to get you ready for your dick." I moan as start stroking my dick while she positions herself on her hands and knees on the floor slowly pushing back against the dildo that's disappeared behind all that ass once she pushes back all the way.

"Hmm shit." She moans. When she leans forwards putting her chest flat on the floor and starts throwing that ass back, I start stroking my shit harder. Seeing her nice round ass rippling at this angle is almost enough to take my backed-up ass the fuck out. My peoples think because they've seen me with women or flirting with them, I've been fucking them but I haven't touched any pussy in over two years. None have piqued my interest the way my angel has since the moment I watched her video after she liked one of mines. She moves it down a little bit then spreads her knees wider and really starts bouncing on that shit. I can't help but to squeeze my shit tighter and twisting my hand the spit I out on my hand giving just enough slippage.

"Fuuuuckkkk." She screams as her breathing gets labored and her movements start to slow alerting to me she just came then I am right behind her. Shooting my seed all over my hand and floor. I grab a napkin from the center console to clean myself and the car floor up. She thinks I am going to be trouble for her but fuck I think it's going to be both ways. I watch her get cleaned up then get back into bed and drift off to sleep.

I sit to watch her sleep a bit before gathering myself to get out the car but my steps are halted when I get an alert of movement outside her home so I switch to the outside back camera and I see the shadow of a person going around the corner of the house in a blind spot. Clearly, I will be installing more cameras around her home because I can't have people being able to find blind spots. I wait to see if any other sensors are triggered but only the front camera is but I still can't quite make out who it is but I can definitely tell it's a man. Welp this nigga clearly has a death wish sneaking around my woman's home. I walk into my house then head to my office so I can pull up all the camera's on the property at once. I have been watching those damn camera's for about a week now every night even while we talk on the phone. I've seen that same shadow twice now just peaking through windows but they haven't tried opening them or the doors. It's been bittersweet watching her cook dinner with lil man or having a movie night with him yesterday not being able to be with my family but soon enough and at least I will get to spend some time with her this weekend. This evening is about the kids but afterwards it's me and her. I take one final look at myself in the mirror and have to admit I look damn good. Most days I have on some version of workout clothes whether it's sweatpants or basketball shorts with a tank top or undershirt on but today's event is formal. I hit up my tailor and he did a brother right as he usually does. This burgundy single button jacket with matching slacks, white dress shirt underneath, black bow tie, and suede loafers were all made just for me. It was all fitted without me looking like I am going to buss out my suit with the wrong movement. Since I decided to stay at my condo above the gym all I need to do is get on my private elevator that opens up in my office. I turn on the tv to check how the event is starting and it's packed already, I even see the mayor has made an appearance. Thankfully my gym is over three thousand square feet so we were able to move most equipment either in the storage room or up against the walls to make room for the tables, bar setup, and the open cook area where the chef is cooking up some of the best hibachi in the city. The moment I step out from the long hallway that leads to my office I am bum rushed by my assistant.

"Ok boss man you have the mayor and a couple of senators that are on campaign runs that want a photo op, of course your parents and brother are here, and your special guest just arrived. Might I say she is drop dead gorgeous too." She gives me what I need to know and the most important thing she said just caught my eye wearing this beautiful black dress with no sleeves, cinched at her waist, with this long split showing off her dipped in chocolate thigh, and all that beautiful hair of hers swept to the side in bouncy curls. My assistant notices where my attention is and struts off to handle more of my business I'm sure. I take the back way to the table she's standing at with her best friend having to stop and shake a few hands before I make it to her. I walk up behind her placing one hand on her waist then lean down to whisper in her ear.

"You look absolutely stunning tonight and smell just as delicious." I whisper then kiss her bare shoulder.

"You look mighty spiffy ya damn self. This color looks good on you." She turns to look up at me and fixes my bow tie. Now that I am closer I can see the light make-up she's wearing but it's the red lips that are making my big man in my pants twitch with joy. She's close enough to feel it and bites on that bottom lip I want to nibble on my damn self.

"Well hello Kairo, I'm Myasia." Mymy introduces herself and I just nod my head at never breaking eye contact with my angel in front of me.

"Hey boss I hate to interrupt but it's time to take those photos and then it's your speech." My assistant walks up to inform me and I almost forgot other people were in the room.

"Right, let me handle this business then it's me and you. Shay move them to my section with my family." I give her kiss on the cheek and firm squeeze on her hip then walk off into the crowd to get this money raised. The center holds a special place with our family as my great grandparents started the center back in the late sixties when the neighborhood was mostly run down homes, they bought up about two blocks of homes over a four year period and fixed them all up for sale but rented out a few to keep in the family. One of those spots is an apartment building that has a hundred apartments that we all still own. Once I get the photo op done with the government flocks which it the most annoying part of my night because we all know those mayonnaise-colored people don't give a damn about our black asses, I head over to the stage we set up in middle of the room.

"Well hello Kairo, it's been a while." Kyla my ex fiancé greets me before I can make it to the stage.

"Kyla I'm not even sure why you are here but I could careless move around, I have a speech to give." I walk around her and make it to the stage but I hear her kiss her teeth behind me. I can't help but chuckle a bit because I don't know what she was thinking even coming here. She broke off our engagement three almost four years ago by leaving a note on my nightstand and clearing all her things out the closet. I need her to understand love doesn't live here anymore and I am all for my angel waiting on me.

"Good evening, family, friends, and valued supporters,

First, let me thank each and every one of you for being here tonight. Your presence alone is a testament to the power of community—and the legacy we are here to protect. In the 1960s, when segregation still cast a long shadow over our neighborhoods, my grandparents dared to dream of something different. They didn't have much, but what they did have was heart, grit, and an unshakable belief in the strength of Black excellence. So, they built a community center—not just a building, but a beacon. That center has stood through riots, recessions, and revitalization. It gave jobs to single mothers, returning citizens, and young men others had already written off. It offered GED prep, trade classes, resume workshops, and coding boot camps before coding was ever cool. We didn't just teach skills—we taught self-worth. Tonight, I ask you to invest not in bricks and mortar but in possibility. In the next generation of leaders, thinkers, builders, and believers. We've come too far to let a legacy like this fade. With your support, we can reimagine what this center can do for our children and their children. Let's make sure the dream that started over 60 years ago doesn't end with us.

Thank you." I raise my champagne glass at the end of my speech and turn to wink at my girl that has the cutest wide smile on her face. I catch a glimpse of Kyla following my line of sight and I walk off stage the moment I see the thought flick on in her head to walk over to my section. I snatch by the arm turning her towards looking around to make sure no one is watching me.

"Don't your lil bird brain ass even think about walking over there messing with my woman. There isn't shit between you and I you made sure of that now leave before you piss me off." I growl out with my jaw tight. She snatches back with a frown on her face then stomps away because she knows my anger better than anyone. I straighten myself up and walk over to my smiling woman who seems to be engrossed in a conversation with my mother.

"Hi ma, pops, and there goes my angel." I greet everyone then sit down next to Arlani since it seems as if Mymy and my brother have engrossed themselves in their own conversation.

"Please tell me this pretty lady here means you're finally settling down cause this one I like." My mom leans forward and points to Arlani between us.

"Yes I am she's your future daughter in law." I reply smiling at my angel who has the deer caught in headlights look on her face.

"Kai why would you tell your mother that." She leans to my side and whispers in my ear.

"Because it's true and you will find out soon enough." I tell her and her cheeks get as red as her dark chocolate skin allows. We talk amongst ourselves for awhile but of course I have to go mingle more with guest after dinner is served. We ended up raising over five hundred thousand dollars for the center that I along with my brother and little sister will make the final decisions on where all of it will go. My big sister will probably join in on a zoom call since she's still in Europe with her family.

"I think those two have hit it off." I lean down behind her chair to whisper in her ear.

"Yea tell me about it she has barely spoke to me all night." She giggles out looking at those two laughing and randomly touching on each other.

"Well I don't want you to leave me yet can you hang around while I get this wrapped up?" I ask her and she nods her head. I give her a kiss on the neck then head to finish up. I look over to the table after saying goodbye to some of the guest and notice Nasir and Mymy have disappeared, so I rush through getting everything else done since my parents have left as well. I have my assistant take Arlani over to my office to wait as we get the last bit of stragglers out the building so the clean-up crew can get to work.

"So my angel do you want to hang out here in my office or checkout my condo upstairs?" I question her after walking into my office to find her admiring some of the paintings I have on the wall.

"Wait you live above your gym?" She looks back at me with a stunned look on her face.

"It's one of my places yes. I usually only stay here when I'm too tired to drive home." I answer her tapping the hidden button for the elevator door to open and I snicker a bit at her expression when it does. I take her hand then step onto the elevator hitting the button for it to go up.

"Your place is beautiful Kai." She smiles looking around at my place. The condo is a bit more modern then my home but it still consist of the same cozy vibe thanks to my sister and mother decorating both for me. I could've done it myself but let's be real why would I when they know me so well and can put all together better.

"So clearly a woman decorated for you. Not that you don't have any style." She stammers over her words a little.

"It's all good baby and by women it was my sister and mother. They do my short-term rental homes as well. It's actually my lil sis business." I explain as I walk into the kitchen to grab a bottle of water for the both of us.

"That's nice. Your little sister and Mymy would be the best of friends then." I walk over to where she's standing in front of the floor to ceiling windows that overlook the cityscape and hand her the cold water. I place mines on the coffee table to take off my suit jacket and bow tie.

"Baby I'm about to get comfortable is that ok?" She nods yes so I head into my room and strip down to my boxers then throw on some basketball shorts and a wifebeater. When I walk back in the living room she has gotten comfortable on the large plush sectional in the living room.

"You good baby?" I ask sitting next to her then stretching my legs out on the long side of the sectional.

"Look I haven't dated in years so I'm hella rusty at this and my life is peaceful. I come in a package with my son so I don't want any unnecessary drama. Are you sure this is what you want?" She turns to me and just blurts out. I appreciate her honesty though and it just further confirms she's my woman.

"We're both rusty and I know we have only been talking seriously for about a week or so but I knew from the moment we started exchanging messages about workouts then different funny videos, and when you popped up on my schedule for one-on-one classes that you were going to be mines. You having your lil man is not a problem for me it's a plus. I love kids and just know I want more he's going to need siblings." I reply looking her right in her eyes to convey my point. She gets shy looking down as she smiles and plays with her curls. I gently lift her head by her chin and connect my lips with hers still tasting some of the champagne on her lips. When she begins kissing me back then straddles my waist I almost lose all control and fuck her so deep and raw our souls are tethered together for centuries but I can't not yet.

"Hmmm baby as much as I want connect our souls forever you're not ready for that yet." I groan trying to picture anything that would make my dick go down before I go against my first mind.

"How do you figure I'm not ready?" She asks still mildly out of breath from our heated make out session.

"Because I can still see some doubt in your eyes and when we make love understand there is no running away, no hiding, no doubt or other people that will keep me from you." She grinds her hips over my dick and I can feel the heat radiating from her pussy and the wetness soaking through her panties.

"You may be right about the doubt so I guess it may be best if I leave, I am definitely going to need my toys tonight." She moans so horny she can barely contain herself.

"I can help you with that. I said I wouldn't make love to you yet that's my dick. I never said anything about my tongue. Get up, take those clothes off, and come sit on my face." I direct her and she moves slowly. Standing, then unzipping her dress and when it falls to the ground she has on nothing but a black laced thong. She turns around to give me full view of that fat ass that I can't wait to see bouncing on my dick then her juicy glistening pussy. I can't help myself so I lean forward, hold her in place my her juicy ass cheeks, then I slowly glide the tip of my tongue from her clit to her entrance licking around it before dipping my tongue inside.

"Mhmm Kai." She moans and clenches her pussy around my tongue inciting my own moan to leave my throat. I suck some of her juices into my mouth then remove my tongue as I sit back and smack her on her voluptuous ass.

"Come sit." I demand as I lay back on the sectional with my head right in the corner so she can rest her knees on the corners. She composes herself and does exactly what I wanted her to do. I grab her thighs to hold her on in place then lick from her entrance to her clit then sucking it between my lips slurping and flicking my tongue against her sensitive bud until her juices are soaking my beard. I release her for a moment.

"K...Kai...Kaiiii." She stutters my name as she leans forward trying to catch her breath and she must think I'm done with her. I slide two of my fingers in her pussy then rub her juices around her back hole slowly pushing my way in. She arches her back moaning in pleasure then grinds her hips against my fingers.

"That's my girl." I groan into her pussy while she continues to rock her hips and we find our rhythm with my fingers going in then out. I flatten my tongue licking side to side against her clit until her juices are raining down my fingers.

"Fuuuuccckk." She screams and begins gasping for air.

"Breath baby." I coach her and she cums again this time squirting all over my tongue and face.

"Oh my... oh my God," She says breathlessly. I remove my fingers licking the ones that were in her pussy then release her other thigh from my grip and she slowly makes her way to sitting on my lap. When we get face to face she pulls me close licking around my mouth then sucking my bottom lip into her mouth and biting on it slightly. I squeeze her bare ass and moan when she licks my bottom lip then slides it across my tongue when I open my mouth. She starts sucking her juices from me and I have to force myself to break the kiss before I go against my word.

"That felt amazing, Kai." She expresses breathing heavily while resting her forehead against mines.

"Come on let's get cleaned up." I instruct her standing from the couch with her legs still wrapped around my waist, my hands under her ass, and her arms around my neck. She has this shocked look on her face making me chuckle at the thought she's never been picked up before. I drop her off in my bathroom, giving her one of my big shirts to wear while I go in my office slash guest bedroom to relieve myself in the shower. When I finally get out I find her sitting on the bench at the foot of my bed using this cocoa butter cream my

sister got me hooked on a while back and I just lean
against the doorframe admiring her natural beauty.

51

Chapter Five

Arlani James

It's been about a month since Kai sucked my soul from my body then put it back with his fingers. I swear if that man can do that with his mouth I am fucked when we have sex. I decided I am going to try this relationship out with him and not just because he can do magic with his tongue either. Ever since that night we have spoken everyday even if it's for brief moment because we're both busy, he sends me lunch because he noticed I tend to over work myself, and not to mention the flowers I've gotten every Monday or his pop ups to cook dinner together. Now that has been beautiful but this bitch Darren is dating is working my last damn nerve. Her test results came back so I had to call her back in the office which she missed the first appointment then finally should up a week later and this bitch had the audacity to say I switched her results to keep her from Darren. Well she's been taking the meds I prescribed her for Trich for about a week now and was due for a check last week but she rescheduled for today. Let's see if she actually comes in but before I can get up to leave my office a knock comes and then the door opens.

"There's the face I've been needing to see all day." Kai greets me the moment he fully enters my office and closes the door behind him. I stand up immediately going into his outstretched arms and he wraps me in his big strong arms. I feel so warm and like nothing can touch me as long as I in them.

"You might've need to see my face but damn I needed this hug." I exhale and then breath in his vanilla, sandalwood, and this other scent I have grown to love so much.

"Well, I am glad I can give you what you need baby. Now who has been upsetting my woman?" He questions kissing the top of my head then he moves to sit in the chair in front of my desk bringing me down on his lap.

"Unfortunately, it's Darren's girlfriend again. She's back for a checkup and I told you how the last one went. I don't know if she just likes bothering me or knows I have the best office in the area and doesn't want to change doctors. She's actually making me consider dropping her as a patient." I confess and actually feel even better as I lay on his chest while he plays with the ends of my braids.

"Well baby you have to protect your peace and I know you mentioned it's even causing strife between you and Zion's father." He reminds me and it's making me lean even further towards dropping her but I think I will try having a talk with the both of them together before I make my final decision.

"I'm over here complaining about my day babe what made you need to see my face so bad you drove an hour and a half in the middle of a work day?" I ask sitting up in his lap and looking him in his eyes that's when I notice the stress written all over his face. I start rubbing his cheek and he kisses the inside of my palm.

"My ex has been causing problems at my gym and just in general. I'm sure she's even been trying to find you but since you're not big on social media like she is she hasn't and I'm sure it would just be to start mess." He explains and I am instantly annoyed. What is it with us being insecure or not knowing when to let the fuck go, well hell men do it sometimes too so I just don't know.

"Well don't worry it's nothing she can tell me that I would believe and I'm sure whatever she's trying to do with the gym will not cause too much trouble. Your work ethic is impeccable." I encourage him while running my hands through locs he decided to let hang looking like curly fries then give him a quick peck on the lips.

"Ms. James your one o'clock is here." My assistant announces over my desk intercom.

"Well here goes nothing, hopefully she's had an attitude readjustment." I exhale but he doesn't let me up until I give him another kiss this one a bit heated.

"I'll be here when you finish and I love seeing you in that white coat baby." He smacks me on the ass as I get up and straighten my dress and coat. I wink at him then leave my office heading to the room they put Farah in and she looks like she has an attitude the moment I walk in.

"Good afternoon, Farah, so today I am just swabbing you for an after-treatment test and will take it from there. So if you will lay back, we can get you tested and on your way." I announce sitting in my seat then prepping myself for the exam. She doesn't say a word but huffs and puffs as she gets into position. We finish everything up and she leaves without another word. I decided to leave early while walking down the hall back to my office and send Darren a text about dinner on Thursday with the four of us to finally settle this shit.

"So Mr. you have me all to yourself. I just took the rest of the day off." I reveal the moment I enter my office and he has this sly grin that spreads across his face then he gets up to hug me.

"Well how about we grab some lunch then take it from there. I've been wanting to try the soul food spot you told me about." He states squeezing my ass inciting a giggle from me.

"Oh one other thing we are having dinner with Darren and his girlfriend Thursday. I hope that's ok."

"Baby whatever you want is cool with me. I was probably going to stay at my crib here anyways. I only have virtual clients this week." I am so glad he's so easy going and secure in himself any other man would've been questioning why or making some damn excuse. We end up having a nice lunch then we went to a rage room to blow off some steam and we had a light dinner. I really wanted that man to turn me every which way but loose but him and his damn restraint. Even though it's technically my week with Zion it's the summer and my parents took him with them to Florida for the next two weeks so I end up home doing some much need self-care with a bottle of wine. Of course, I texted my man between reading this new book I found online. Thursday got here quicker than I expected it to and now I'm in here slaving over a hot stove with my man helping me but distracting me at the same time.

"Babe stop it. You're going to make me burn the chicken." I laugh out as he keeps kissing on my neck or rubbing my ass.

"I can't help it you and this damn sundress then you over here smelling like coconut and mangos. Real lickable and shit." He groans in my ear and his deep voice makes me glad I didn't wear any panties just in case he gets hungry. We may not have had sex yet but that man's appetite for eating my pussy is like a man who hasn't had a meal in years. I decided on some country eating tonight so I'm frying some chicken wings, the mac and cheese is in the oven with the cornbread, and I made cabbage with ham hocks instead of collard greens for Kai. Kai sets my round breakfast table since it's only the four of us while I start placing the food on serving trays. I swear we move in unison like we've been together for years and I love it for me.

"Ok babe they are pulling up." I announce after looking at the security panel on the island and I see his car pull behind Kai's. I walk to open the door as Kai put's the food on the table.

"Hi Darren, Farah." I greet them both cordially even if I want to smack Darren for bringing this stupid bitch into our lives but hopefully now that she see's me happily with Kairo she will ease the fuck up.

"Darren this is Kairo. Kai this Zion's father and his girlfriend Farah." I introduce them and Kai shakes Darren's hand. I notice the difference between their sizes immediately. Kai is at least six inches taller than Darren and let's not even mention the muscle size. Damn my man is fucking huge. I see how Farah is looking at him and this bitch must want me to knock her head between the fridge and the cabinet. Darren has this jealousy look in his eyes and I don't get why. These two are rubbing me the wrong way and they just stepped in the damn door.

"OK y'all the food is done and the wine is on the table but if you want something else just let me know." I try to break the tension in the room because we not doing this shit tonight. We take a seat and start to eat but I notice Farah barely grabs any food.

"Damn baby this food taste amazing." Kai compliments my dinner. The last time he was here and we cooked dinner it was a shared thing this one is all me. He leans over to kiss me on my cheek and I can't help but cheese.

"It's ok. A lil salty for my taste." Farah complains and turns her nose up then moves the mac and cheese around on her plate.

"Ok that's it I've tried to be nice to your ass. What's your problem with me?" I snap dropping my fork down on my plate and Kai grabs my thigh then slightly squeezes it to calm me.

"I already told you. You're a controlling bitter baby mama and now I think you just want to have them both to yourself." She snaps back and I am still at a lost.

"Farah, I told you to chill on that mess. She's not controlling a damn thing." Darren chastises her and his brown skin starts turning red.

"Exactly we made decisions when our son was a baby how things would go since we didn't work out and we tried the relationship thing there wasn't a romantic bone in my body for him. He's a great friend and father nothing more." I say that to also make sure Kai understands our relationship as well and he recognizes that.

"Baby I'm good. I know where you want to be and I can't wait to meet little Zion when you're ready." He states then pulls me close by my chin to give me a kiss with his soft moist lips. When he releases me, I catch that look from Darren and I'm not sure this is the best time to address it but clearly Kai does.

"Darren it's cool if you still have feelings for her but she doesn't for you so keep that shit clean. It's probably why ya girl acting the way she is. Instead of checking you she pointing that shit at my woman and I won't have y'all disturbing her peace with ya bullshit." He gets on him and plants him with a stern look but Darren looks like he's just been caught. I realize now that he may actually have feelings for me and it's making me mad because he never said anything.

"Wait a damn minute Darren is he right? Do you have feelings for me?" I ask looking over at him and he puts his head down.

"Look I didn't mean to catch feelings for you I just did. That night was more than a drunk night for me and I've been trying to wait to see if you had any for me but you never came around so I tried moving on." He confesses and now I'm sitting here playing all our interactions making sure I wasn't leading him on in any way.

"Well I'm glad you moved on. So can you chill the hell out chick? He's with you and I am with Kai." She just nods her head but she still has this look in her eyes that I can't quite tell what it is. We end dinner and they leave.

"Ok well now that all that mess is over." Kai comes up behind me wrapping his arms around my waist as we sway to the beat of the song I have playing. I turn around then tiptoe to give him a kiss that he happily obliges.

"I'm ready Kairo. I'm all yours." I say against his lips and he picks me up by my ass. I wrap my legs around his waist and he walks us to my bedroom without another word. Our tongues begin a heated dance the moment we get into my room only stopping to pull my dress over my head and his shirt then dropping his slacks along with his boxers. When he lays me on the bed and I see his dick for the first time I damn near choke on my own spit. He should be the picture in the ebonics dictionary for a man with a third leg. I mean it's so thick, long, and pretty if it's possible for a mans dick to be pretty.

"Baby… I need you to be sure you're ready for this because when I look at you, feel you, everything in me settles. Connecting to you in this way will be like the last piece of my soul clicking into place. And once I slide into this wet shit there's no backing out, no leaving. If we argue, we're going to talk it out grown, real, and respectful because love doesn't mean we'll never clash, it means we'll never give up. Understand I'm your provider emotionally, physically, and spiritually. Your protector, even if what I'm protecting you from is your own overthinking or my own pride. You are mine. And I am yours. So last chance." He groans with his hard dick in his hand so close to my entrance I know he can feel how wet he just made me with his confession.

"I don't know how it's possible in such a short time, but I feel that you are serious in every bone in my body and while it's scary it's what I want as long as it's from you. So enter your pussy baby." I advise wrapping my legs around his waist to pull him closer and the moment his head enters my pussy I arch my back off the bed and my breath gets caught in my throat.

"Ummm fuck baby you're so tight breath and relax for me. Hmm shit that's it. Ooooh fuck." He leans forward and growls in my ear. I mean full on growls causing my pussy to get even wetter and clench around his rock hard dick that's stretching my pussy for dear life.

"Kai... Kaiiii right there." I moan as my juices rain down his dick.

"Now that you've got that first nut out the way. You better not cum again until I tell you to. You hear me?" He demands sitting up halfway then places his hand around my neck and my pussy pulses on its on accord. I nod yes because I am too fucking stunned right now. I've never had a man talk to me like that or put his damn hands around my neck.

"Use your words Lani."

"Ye.. yes I hear you Kai but you feel so good babe." I moan while moving my hips to get some friction since he's stopped stroking my brain cells loose.

"You will or no more dick for you." He counters and I pout. He leans forward kissing me with more passion than ever before and I swear I want to cum just from that alone. This man has me opened like an exposed nerve that he controls and can send off with one touch. He sits up fully resting on his calves then pulls me closer pushing my legs back with his hands on the back of my thighs and has my pussy fully exposed to him.

"Hmmm your pussy looks so good wrapped around my dick." He moans as he starts thrusting in and out and I try to concentrate on anything but how good he feels so I don't cum.

"Take those pretty ass tittes out and play with them baby." He commands. I unclip my bra from the front and my triple D's spill out with my nipples already hard and sensitive. I lick two of my fingers on either hand and begin to rubs circles around my nipples. When I do he pushes in so fucking deep it feels like he tapping my damn uterus then pulls out to his tip.

"Ka...Kai.. plea... please." I stutter attempting to plead with him but not being able to get the words out.

"Please Kai what? Talk to me baby tell me what my lil slut needs. Oooh you like being called my lil slut huh." He taunts me slowing his strokes but still so fucking deep.

"I.. I need to cum Kai please." I beg finally able to form a damn sentence.

"Nope not yet. Keep taking this dick like a big girl." He taunts me further while he speeds up his strokes keeping them short this time then going back deep and snapping his hips forward each time.

"Fuuucckkk. Kai babe pleas...please. Your slut needs to cum sooo bad." I moan and I feel his dick twitch inside me.

"That's my good lil slut beg for me. Cum... For... Me." He thrust with each word and my orgasm washes over me so hard I feel light headed and he strokes me through it.

"Look at the mess your making all over your dick baby." He grunts releasing my thigh with one hand then placing that hand behind my head to make me look at where his dick is stroking my pussy. I can't help but moan then clench my walls around his dick until I find a rhythm with his strokes.

"Ka... Kaiii baby please can I cum pleassee." I moan feeling another orgasm trying to wash over me.

"Cum and keep those pretty eyes open and on me." This time when I cum I don't just cream all over his dick I squirt all over us and it must do something to him because he release the back of my neck then grabs me around the front. He squeezes just enough to make it a little hard to breath then leans forward.

"Say your mines." He demands in a low growl next to my ear.

"I... I'm yours Kairo. Fuck I'm all yours." I scream as my orgasm hits me and I feel his warm cum shoot into me causing my orgasm to keep going until I see stars. I feel like something shifts in me when he lifts up with his hand still around my neck still stroking me through both our nuts and looks me in my eyes.

"You felt it didn't you?" He asks me still staring into my eyes and the crazy thing is I did that last nut was so euphoric.

"Yes, I did. I've never felt anything like that before." I confess to him as he slides out of me and I feel so empty.

"Of course you haven't. That was meant for me and me only baby. Come on let's get cleaned up." He gives me a kiss on the lips then gets out the bed and picks me up once he plants his feet to the floor. That man takes my loofa and soap then scrubs my body from the neck down. He even knew to grab my rag to clean my lady parts. Once he got himself cleaned up and we got out he also massage my body butter all over me before we laid down in the bed with fresh seats at that.

Chapter Six

Kairo Levi

These past few weeks after connecting with my angel has truly been fucking heaven for me. Being up in that pussy has been everything short of magical dammit. She caught on to my dominate ways in the bed and has listened very well. She even let me tie her to her bed and blindfold her during sex. I got to meet lil Zion last week and he is the coolest little boy and a badass on that soccer field. I met him at his last soccer practice. In other news whoever was snooping around has noticed my presence and only showed up once. I ordered an upgrade in her security system, and they are coming out this evening to install everything. I just finished up my last class for today and am heading to my condo upstairs to get showered as well as changed into something casual since we are going out with Zion to the game room.

"What the fuck are you doing in my office Kyla?" I roar in frustration because for whatever reason she has been on my ass lately.

"That's no way to greet your wife, well soon to be at least." She replies and I have to rub my eyes to make sure I'm seeing clear because I swear this bitch grew two fucking heads just now. I've seen delusional people before but how the fuck did I get in the crosshairs of one. I mean I haven't seen this bitch in over three years now the moment I get me someone here she goes.

"Look I am going to give you one last chance to walk out on your own. I've already told you I want nothing to do with your ass. Especially now that I'm with someone so just gone on somewhere." I groan stepping back out my office to signal for my assistant to come over.

"I know I messed up Kaikai but I missed you and I want to fix what we had. I was childish to run off like that knowing how much I loved you." She stands from sitting on my desk and starts to walk over to me like what she just confessed is going to sway me.

"Kyla you must think I'm some dumb lame ass nigga if you thought that was going to work on me. I know why you really left me. I found out about buddy you cheated on me with and you thought he had more bread than me and was going to take care of your lazy ass, but he tricked your ass literally. Even if I didn't know about why you left me, I'm happy with my woman and there ain't shit you can say or do." I back up further as she tries to reach for me, but my sister comes out of nowhere, grabs her hand then pushes her back and she falls on the floor dramatically.

"Bitch keep your hands off my brother he has told ya ass he's done with you so move around before I fuck you up." She threatens her and I can't help but laugh. Kyla is no match for my little sister; I trained her my damn self on top of what my father required growing up.

"Sis can you deal with this? I need to get showered and ready to head to Lani."

"Of course, tell Lani I can't wait to see her at family dinner and meet that handsome little boy of hers." She agrees then rubs in the fact that she likes Arlani and she never liked Kyla's ass. I've been asking myself what the hell did I even see in her ass. I mean the broad has no damn drive to do anything but spend money and look cute for social media.

"Now back to you. Ya shit for brains, bleach blond, black N' mild lookin cum bucket it's time for ya to exit stage left." Ayoki shouts as she grabs Kyla by the legs and drags her out of my office while she's kicking and screaming. I damn near choke on my spit laughing at the shit she called her. I hop in my big boi GMC pickup and head to get my family to have some fun but my phone rings before I can even get on the road good.

"Hi, my angel I'm on my way to y'all now." I greet her.

"That's great babe but is there something you want to tell me before you get here?" She questions me.

"Nope not that I can think of." I decide to play forgetful.

"Kai did you order an upgrade to my security system?" She huffs out and I can't help but laugh because my woman is fiercely independent but hey I warned her who I am.

"Maybe, maybe not. Would it be such a bad thing if I did?"

"No, I guess not but babe this thing had to cost you a fortune. The four-k night vision camera's alone are worth a couple thousand dollars not to mention the sensors, floodlights, smoke and carbon dioxide alarms, and the list keeps going." She lists out just some of the upgrades I ordered.

"Babe I would pay what I did tenfold to make sure you and lil man are safe. What did I tell you?" I ask just to see how coherent her horny ass was our first night.

"That you are my provider and protector in every way possible. I wasn't completely delirious yet." She jokes and I just smile.

"Well, are they almost done? I should be there in about forty-five minutes. I know big man is ready to play his games." I check with her.

"Yea they are and don't remind me. He has been bouncing off the walls excited since I told him you were taking us. I think he likes you." She reveals and that has a nigga feeling all warm in the chest. We talk for a few more minutes then end the call. Just as I promised I pulled up forty-five minutes later and leave the truck running since I know they are ready.

"Hi beautiful and Zi you ready to have some fun my boy?" I greet them once they come to the door.

"I'm so ready they have a new ninja turtle game I wanted to play." He answers so excitedly and gives me a high five. I take the stool out of the backseat that I bought for them both so he can hop in the backseat and then I help my baby get in. We run around for hours with little man wanting to try every game in the place we even did the rock-climbing wall, and this dinosaur virtual reality game.

"I don't think I've seen him this worn out unless he's been to one of his soccer games. He really had fun tonight." She expresses as I buckle him into the backseat using the blanket I have as a makeshift pillow and put the rest over him just in case he gets cold then help my angel inside.

"It was fun for me too and I thought I could eat wings. I think he almost ate his weight in them." I chuckle once I get settled in my seat and start up the truck.

"He wasn't too much for you, was he? You can be honest." She seems to be feeling unsure.

"Baby I had the most fun with you two tonight then I've had in years. If the kids, we have together one day are half as cool as my Zi then I'll be the happiest dad on this earth. I'm just glad he had fun with me." I assure her as I grab her hand and bring it to my lips for a kiss while I steer the truck with the other hand. She just smiles keeping ahold of my hand and gets comfortable in her seat.

"Hey baby we made it back to the house." I coax her awake by rubbing her cheek with the back of my hand and she starts coming to.

"Dang, I don't even remember falling asleep. Oh, I gotta wake him up to bathe." She turns to look at a still sleeping Zion.

"Ok well I will carry him in the house and turn the shower on for you while you get him awake." I offer as I get out the truck to go around to their side to help her out.

"Oh, babe you don't have to. I'm sure you're tired yourself." I just look at her sideways as I pick up Zion out the backseat. She turns to get the door open as I come up the stairs with him and we head upstairs to his room. He starts to wake up when I rub his back and call his name, so I stand him up next to Lani.

"Anything special he likes to sleep in?" I ask.

"No just grab anything, thanks." She replies and I grab his things then go into his en suite bathroom to get his shower ready. I wink at her as I head out of the room and she smiles.

"Really thank you for the help just now babe." She says tiptoeing to give me a kiss that I happily give her.

"Glad I can help but you look exhausted baby. Go ahead and get yourself cleaned up too, I will head out." I tell her as I rub her cheek.

"You sure baby? I can stay up with you for a bit."

"I'm sure. I will check on you two in the morning. Come on and set this alarm." I usher her to the front door after giving her a tight hug and another kiss. Once I hear the alarm say armed, I get in my truck to head to my home here which is only about twenty minutes away from her thankfully because I am tired. When I get about five minutes from the house, I notice some alerts on my phone and decide to check them since I'm stopped at a red light. When I see the alert for after we left of some nigga walking into the back sliding door, I bus an immediate U-turn because I never see this muthafucka leave. I feel so stupid I didn't check the house before leaving. I try calling her phone twice but get no answer and my heart rate doubles.

"Please... Please God let me make it there in time." I begin to plead as I am flying down the road back to her house. I reach there in half the time slamming on breaks the moment I get close to her driveway throwing my truck in park and not even bothering to cut the truck off. I don't even bother with knocking. I use the door code to let myself in and purposely not hit the alarm. I pull out my gun from my waistband the moment I hear her scream. I take the steps two at a time and buss into her bedroom door to find the bitch ass nigga Chance she had the date with standing behind her with a knife to her throat, his other hand over her mouth, her hands are zip tied, and she still has the same clothes on she went out in.

"It's going to be ok baby." I assure her as I point the gun at that bitch ass nigga's head.

"Just move out the way or I will slit her throat." He threatens moving to the right but she trips him, so I shot him once in the shoulder, the other in the chest and he falls to the floor. I rush over to grab her from so close to him then pull my pocketknife out to cut the zip ties.

"Shit baby are you ok did he hurt or touch you?" I rapid fire off questions as I look over her body for any visible signs.

"Mommyyy." Zion shouts running to her in my arms as we sit on the floor. The alarm blaring is what woke him and I'm glad he didn't see his mom in that position.

"She's ok lil man." I assure him as I rub his back while she holds him with tears streaming down her face.

"Police call out." They announce when they come in the house and I yell that we are upstairs. They come up with guns pointed.

"Hey man put that shit down it's a child right here the person you're after is over there. He probably needs an ambulance." I inform them and one of them calls for one over their walkie talkie. I have them question me downstairs and have them let her take Zion back into his room until a female officer is able to question her because I seen the look in her eyes when the male officer approached her. She was able to get Zion to stay in his room with Mymy once she came over after hearing all the commotion from the police cars pulling in.

"Can he stay with me, please." She asks the female officer as she stands. at my side with her arms wrapped around my waist and head buried into my side.

"If that's what you need to be comfortable, sure. Now can you tell me what happened."

"We..We-" She starts but can't get anything out and starts to panic.

"It's ok baby take a deep breath for me." I coach her through some breaths to calm her and after a few attempts she calms enough to speak.

"We had just come home from hanging out with my boyfriend Kai here. He had left to go home while I got ready for bed. When I came out the bathroom to go to get some clothes, I... I found Chance standing in the middle of my room with this crazed look in his eyes. Before I could scream or do anything he jumped on me and we wrestled on the floor for a bit but then he pulled the kn...knife out to put at my neck then started to put the zip ties on me. I heard the front door, so I screamed when he moved the blade from my neck when we were getting up off the floor." She pauses and I tune out the rest but try to continue to comfort her since the rest of the story I already know. The police didn't charge me with anything since it was clear in defense of Arlani but only after they checked me for warrants, my gun being legal, and the security footage. They wheeled him off to the nearest hospital while questioning us.

"Is there anywhere you can stay until the CSI team finishes collecting evidence?" The officer inquires and I don't want to assume this time that she wants to stay with me so I let her answer.

"Yes I'll stay with my boyfriend." She answers and I say a silent thank God because I didn't want to fight with her tonight about that.

"Ok you will be notified when they have cleared out." Mymy somehow got Zion to go back to sleep so I pick him up from the bed while they grab a few things for him and we head to my place.

"Baby go shower you can wear some of my clothes." I instruct her after putting Zion in my bed then I walk to turn the shower on for her.

"Can you stay in here with us tonight?" She pleads with her eyes.

"Whatever you need from me baby." I assure her as I pull her into my arms then kiss the top of her head. When I hear her crying in the shower, I wish I would've done everything in silence so I could torture that nigga slowly. I lean my head against the closed door, but I know she needs to let it out, so I just wait for her at the door. When she finally comes out, I wrap her in my arms and she continues to silently cry.

"I got you baby, always." I rock her side to side kissing the top of her head and she soon calms down enough to put on the clothes I gave her then get into bed.

"I'm getting in the shower. I will leave the door open, just holler if you need me, ok." I move her hair out her face and kiss her on the forehead. She nods her head then rolls over to wrap her arms around a sleeping Zion. I quickly get cleaned up, dressed and get in bed wrapping my arm around her.

"It's just me baby go back to sleep." I whisper in her ear when she flinches from my touch but then relaxes when she realizes it's me and eventually falls back to sleep.

Chapter Seven

Arlani James

Waking up the next morning after Chance tried to take me from my home, I'm in a panic because I wake up with Zion and Kai nowhere to be seen but then I hear laughter down the hall I recognize as my baby boy. When I get out the bed then start to walk to the door, I begin to smell bacon and eggs the closer I get to the kitchen.

"Well, something smells good in here." I announce my presence once I step into Kai's large modern kitchen that's fit for a chef.

"Mom look Mr. Kai is letting me do the pancakes." He says excitedly flipping a pancake on the griddle.

"I showed him how to do it a couple of times, and he got the hang of it pretty fast." Kai says looking like a proud dad standing next to Zion as he scrambles the eggs on the other end. I take a seat at the island to watch my two favorite men make me breakfast. It's not a better way to spend my morning after the night I had. I still can't believe Chance really tried to kidnap me last night. He just kept going on and on about me being his big ticket and how I ruined everything for him.

"Babe you, ok?" Kai questions me standing right next to me and I didn't even realize he had stopped cooking.

"Um hmm. I just zoned out for a minute." I tell him not wanting to get into what all Chance really said to me. He hugs me tight, and it feels so damn good I relax instantly then lay my head on his chest. He kisses the top of my head while we watch Zion finish up the last few pancakes. They plate our food, and we eat in a comfortable silence with Kai occasionally rubbing my thigh when he notices me zoning out. When we're all done, I make them go get washed up while I cleaned the kitchen.

"I told him he could play in the pool if it's ok with you." Kai tells me as he walks up behind me and wraps his arms around me while I stand at the sink looking out the window at the pool.

"Yea he can get in. I grabbed some of his basketball shorts when I picked out his clothes." I hear his big feet running down the hall then he flies out the sliding glass doors Kai opened when I gave him the green light. I decide to go sit in one of his lounge chairs near the pool, maybe the sun will do me some good. I lay there with my eyes close listening to Kai dunk Zion in the pool and him laughing hysterically. Now this is how my weekends should be. He has an array of pool toys out and I remember he has a few nieces and nephews from his older sister. Then something else hits me.

"Kai... Kai." I yell and he finally hears me. As he steps out of the pool, water streaming down his body, I can't help but let my gaze linger. The sun caresses every sculpted muscle, his chest glistening, abs taut and defined, droplets tracing the deep grooves between each line. His broad shoulders taper down to arms strong enough to make anyone feel safe, and his thick, powerful thighs flex with every stride, the kind you want wrapped around you. Even his calves are cut and solid, every inch of him radiating strength and raw magnetism. I bite my lip almost forgetting what I wanted to ask him as the heat coils low in my belly, still unable to tear my eyes away from the pure, physical poetry of a man before me.

"Yes baby, everything ok?" He questions while whipping his face with the towel he grabbed from a room on the back of the house.

"Yea I just remembered something. How did you know something was wrong and how did you get in the house?" I turn to look at him sitting next to me now and he looks down at his hands reminding me of Zion when he's done something he's not supposed to.

"Baby please understand something. I've only ever wanted to protect you and be there for you from the moment we started sharing videos in our DM's. That feeling only became worse when we started our one on one's and I noticed the way you looked at me like you liked me too." He says as he beats around the bush.

"Kairo you are beginning to make me scared about what you're about to say. Just spit it out." I demand sitting up in my seat now.

"I have access to the cameras in your house, and I know the code to the door, always have." He looks up at me with fear in his eyes and I can only imagine mines mirror his because did this man just tell me he has always had access to my camera's.

"How the hell have you always had access to my cameras Kai?" I whisper yell trying not to alert Zion who is playing happily in the pool.

"Well you know Nasir owns a tech company, and he can pretty much gain access to anything. Before we started really talking I had him hack your cameras and put a file together on you. Last night I received an alert that your sliding door had opened while we were out, but I didn't notice it until I was on my way home and when I watched it to see if the person ever left I noticed they didn't, so I bussed a U-turn to get back to you. I know it's not the norm but-"

"No, it's not normal for you to basically stalk me before we even started dating Kairo. What the fuck.. I can't believe this shit. The moment I decide to date I run into two crazy ass men. No don't touch me Kairo." I yell standing from my seat by accident, and I am happy Zion is swimming under water, so he didn't hear me.

"Please baby don't be mad. I would never hurt you. I just had to see for myself you were who I thought you were before I put myself out there again." He pleads.

"Mad is not the height of my feelings right now Kairo. You invaded my damn privacy. How can you not see the wrong in that?" I groan sitting back down and rubbing my hands through my hair trying to figure out how my life has taken such a crazy ass turn.

"I'm so sorry I just couldn't be lied to or end up left again." He confesses with his head down and I've never seen him look so defeated. He always has this air of confidence and strength, but can I really excuse what he did.

"Kairo I don't know. I... I need to go home where's my phone." I stutter getting up again and walking into the house.

"Baby please don't leave and go back to that house yet. Besides Zion is enjoying himself. If it's me you want to be away from, I will leave. For your mental just don't go back there yet." He begs then reaches out to me, but I move away again. I swear I see his heart break in his eyes, but I can't trust this man if he will do something so crazy as to hack my damn cameras or running a background check on me and heavens knows what else he's done. A part of me wants to ask what else he has done and the other is absolutely terrified at what else he might've done. Now that I stop for a moment I realize he's right. It wouldn't be a good idea for me to go back home yet.

"Ok I will stay here for a bit, but you need to leave and prove you've shut off all these cameras. You've invaded my privacy enough." I snap just thinking about it all again. He sighs and pulls out a tablet from the nightstand and turns it towards me then opens an app that has all these cameras outside label as well as a few inside. He hands it to me then writes something on a sticky not he pulls from the drawer as well and hands that to me. I read the note and it's his login information.

"I love you Arlani and I really am sorry. You and Zion can stay here as long as you like but just know I'm not giving up on us. I'm just giving you some space." He declares and as much as I don't want to feel all warm and fuzzy I do after what he says. He grabs his keys then walks out of the room. I hear him tell Zion he would see him later and then I hear the front door open and close. When I turn my phone it's flooded with messages from Mymy, Darren, and even my parents. I call my parents to ease their minds first, but I don't tell them about Kairo for some reason. I just send a text to Darren to let him know we're ok and staying away from the house right now. I notice a voicemail from an unknown number and after listening to it, I find out that they are done with my house, so I look up a cleaning service and call Mymy.

"Oh my gosh bitch is you ok? Where are you?"
She blurts out question after question when she
answers.

"I'm ok I guess and I'm at Kairo's house. I will
send you the address, but I scheduled for a cleaning
service to come for my bedroom can you bring me some
clothes and watch them when they get there."

"Of course I can. I'm still trying to wrap my head
around everything. Like your man is about that life. He
really shot a nigga about you." She murmurs but notices
I get quiet when she mentions him shooting Chance.

"I'm sorry girl look text me what time they will be
here and the address. I will text you once they are done
and I am on my way. I love you girl." She says.

"I love you too. The messages are sent." I inform
her then end the call. I sit on the edge of the bed holding
my phone and the tablet Kairo gave me then I turn off
the cameras. I notice he's texted me to let me know
there are keys to one of his cars in the garage if I want to
go out and I can't help but smile. I go back downstairs
and spend the day with Zion in the pool. My phone
starts ringing and I answer it without looking completely
distracted from the video of Kairo working at in his home
gym.

"Lani are you sure your ok? I can come by and be
with you guys?" Darren rushes out the moment I answer
the phone. I hope his other feelings aren't what's

motivating his ass right now because I am not in the mood to be nice.

"Darren I texted and told you we were fine. Kairo handled everything. Zion didn't even see anything, he just heard the gunshot and Kairo busting in my room to save me." I groan starting to catch an attitude with him interrupting my Kairo show and the moment the thought forms I have to laugh at myself a little.

"Thank God for Kairo." He says sarcastically and I just shake my head then pop a pineapple in my mouth. He has so much fresh fruit in his fridge it's like a damn farmers market.

"Look do you want to talk to Zion or something? He should be out the shower, he's been playing in the pool all day and not to long ago fed his face." I ask him in a hurry to get him off the phone.

"No it's ok let him relax. I will see him tomorrow night. Just send me the address where you are." This nigga working my nerves now.

"No need, Mymy will be at the house with him. She should actually be here in a few to get him." I'm still wondering was it a good idea to have him go back tonight but I need to be alone and process everything.

"OK well have a good night then." He sounds so pitiful when I end the call. Ms. Farah must not be there with him which would be a shocker the way she's up his ass. By the time I get the fruit put away Zion is running down the hall and Mymy is ringing the doorbell so I go open the door.

"Awww bestie." She says dramatically wrapping me up in a hug that I gladly return.

"I'm ok Mymy." I admit as we walk over to the living room to sit down.

"Hi Goddy baby. You ok?" She asks Zion while giving him a hug.

"Yes, I got to play in Mr. Kairo big pool. He has so many cool toys for it, even played with me for a while but then he had to go." He rambles on and I see the disappointment in his eyes that Kairo left.

"Sounds fun but I'm sure he had to do something important because who wouldn't want to play with my favorite cookie monster." She says tickling him and he balls up laughing.

"Now go in the room and give me and your mom a bit to talk then we will head out." He nods his head and takes off back to Kairo's game room down the hall to play video games. I know the look she's giving me and I'm sure she caught the tone in my voice earlier when I mentioned Kairo. We sit and I run everything down to her from the moment Chance jumped on me to finding out what Kairo did.

"Damn woman that's a lot but can I be real with you for a minute?" I know whatever her ass is about to say I am not going to like it.

"Like no one else in my life woman."

"I know it's a bit unorthodox what he did but let's be real a man with the type of money he clearly has and from what you told me about his ex fiancé can you really blame him. I mean the girl made it seem like she was in school and using social media to make money whole time she's jumping from one rich nigga to the next to pay her bills plus she was never even in school. She only left him because she thought the dude she was creeping with had more money than him whole time he just doesn't flaunt his shit like these other niggas." She breaks the shit down and I can't help but start thinking I might've over reacted a little.

"So you telling me you wouldn't find it creepy that a man hacked the camera's in your home to watch you without you knowing?" I ask her for clarification.

"If it was some random weirdo yes but a nigga that I'm interested in anyways, ehh not so much. Oh and let's not forget one major fact. If he wasn't in your security system you would probably be dead or some fat rich nigga sex slave from what you said Chance kept repeating. Another thing he could've lied to you but instead he told you the truth and was still trying to take care of you by keeping you from that damn house for a bit longer for your damn mental." I swear I have a love hate relationship with how real my bestie is but the fact is she's right and I hate it.

"I guess you're right. Shit I even found myself watching him work out in his home gym before you got here. He gave me the password to his system earlier to turn the cameras off in here." I confess leaning my head back on the sofa.

"Well damn how many houses does he have? This place is nice as hell alone especially with the size of the yard I can see out those doors." She looks around at where we're sitting and where we are you can see the dining room, kitchen as well as the back yard.

"According to his security system four in total but he does rent this one out as a short term and the same for the condo over his gym. You think this is nice the Montgomery house is two stories and sitting on about six acres but the other location I haven't been there yet."

"I caught that yet heffa. All jokes aside though I get the privacy issue but don't lose out on your forever because he doesn't play by the same societal rules you're use to. That man has shown he's willing to provide, protect and be real with you."

"Ugh you're right but I need some time and enough about me what's going on with you and Nasir? Don't think I haven't noticed he's the only car I've seen over there for the past month." I question her and the smile that spreads on my bestie face makes my heart smile too.

"Welllllll those brothers are definitely a different breed of men but he is a sweetheart, smart as hell, and damn that man is delicious." She fans herself and I can't help but giggle along with her. We sit there talking about her day at the boutique, her date last night before all hell broke loose, and played a few rounds of Street Fighter with Zion before they prepared to leave.

"Bestie are you sure you're going to be ok here alone?" She looks at me concerned.

"I turned the camera's back on while Zi was packing his bag. As mad as I am and still a bit weirded out I feel safer knowing he's probably watching over me." I confess looking up at the camera by the front door and smiling.

"Good now I don't feel bad about leaving you here cause he will be here in two shakes of a tail feather about you." She laughs and so do I. I hug her and Zion again then lock up the house. I head straight for Kai's glass wine room across from the formal dining room and grab a chilled bottled of merlot then grab a wine glass from the shelf in the room. I'm not sleepy yet to I head to the kitchen, make me some popcorn, pop the cork, and head to the living room to watch a movie. I grab one of his throw blankets and get comfortable then eventually fall asleep.

Chapter Eight

Kairo Levi

It's been about three days since my angel decided to stop speaking to me and I am in the gym trying to burn some energy and clear my mind as well as keep me from going over there.

"Bro she still hasn't spoken to you yet?" Nasir questions walking into his home gym since I've been staying at the house he has in Birmingham. Him and Mymy have hit it off and probably about to go on another date tonight I assume with the way he's dressed.

"No man and I have texted and called her. Hell I even sent her favorite lunch to her job and those damn people don't even deliver." I exhale and rant dropping down from the pull up bar I was just working on.

"From what my love has told me she had a pretty stressful day at the clinic. Somebody popped up and laid something heavy on her."

"Wait who the hell popped up on my woman? Man fuck this I'm going over there. She clearly not as mad as she was she turned the camera's on for me to watch her." I start throwing my shit in my bag when Nasir stops me.

"Bru I want you to get your girl, but you scared her once just give her time." He tries to calm me but I don't think I can after hearing someone popped up on her in her place of business which means they've been looking for her.

"Look me and Myasia are having some late-night drinks, I will get some info from her just wait by your phone cause I'm not coming back tonight." He daps me up and leaves. He's right, even though I will not agree out loud but fuck this patient shit is killing me. I look at the time and realize it is after ten so I just head up to get showered and find something to eat. When I hop out the shower I hear my phone ringing so I rush to it hoping it's my angel finally deciding to call and it actually is. I don't say anything at first but then I hear what sounds like sniffles.

"Baby what's wrong? Talk to me." I plead when I hear her crying harder.

"If you don't answer me, I am coming to you." I warn.

"Please come." She wails and I am throwing on clothes and shoes in record time.

"I'm on my way baby." I say and she ends the call. Nasir's home is only ten minutes away from my crib so I'm there in no time. When I walk in the house it is pitch dark and I hear her cries coming from my room. My heart rate picks up thinking she may be in danger again so I also pull my gun out this time I quietly move through the house to my room. The door is cracked open so I slowly push it further and find her balled up in the bed. When I step in and realize no ones actually in the room with her I rush over to where she is laying to rub her back and she flinches but looks up at me then launches herself in my direction, so I wrap my arms around her.

"Ooooh baby what happened?" I try to soothe her by rubbing her back as I stand with her wrapped around me like an octopus. I sit on the bed rocking her while still rubbing her back as if she was a baby but it seems to be working because her tears and sniffle slow down.

"I... I had a nightmare and the only person I wanted was you." She says into my shoulder finally calming down completely.

"I'm happy to be here baby. Do you want to talk about the nightmare?" She nods her head and sits up but doesn't move off my lap.

"First I have to say this I still don't know if I can fully accept what you did but I'm not mad. I turned the cameras back on because I do feel safer knowing you are watching over me or getting alerts if something happens and-" She pauses taking a deep breath and looks down at her hands resting between us.

"I love you too Kairo. I am not even sure it's possible to love someone so quick but I know how I feel." She finally looks up at me so I slowly pull her face to me and connect our lips in a slow but quick kiss then lean my forehead against hers.

"It was only a few days but not hearing from you was pure agony there wasn't a workout I could do to clear you from my mind but I understand why you needed it." She gives me another kiss and takes a deep breath gearing up to tell me what this nightmare was all about and hopefully who the fuck thought it was smart to pop up on her to disrupt her day.

"Well the dream was about what I was told today by a surprise visitor at the clinic and I'm sure you already know I had one by the look on your face. It wasn't a bad person Kai what they told me just was." She giggles then rubs her finger between my brows that are damn near touching because I became even more irritated.

"You remember the night I had the date with Chance. Our waitress that night was acting weird as hell towards him and I thought it was an ex or something but I found out who she really was-" She starts to tell me but then her phone starts to ring and she leans to grab it while still sitting in my lap. She answers it on speaker when she sees that it's Darren calling.

"Darren is everything ok it's late." She asks the moment she answers.

"I want my mommy. Ok son I have her on the phone now give me a second." I hear him try to hush Zion then a door sliding open and closed.

"Darren why is my baby crying for me?" She stands going into a panic. I walk to the closet smiling at her hanging her clothes in my closet and grab one of her dresses since she's in some boy shorts and tank top. I grab some slides on my way out and hand them to her. In the middle of her panic she smiles at me and that just what I wanted to give her.

"There was an accident earlier tonight and he burned himself with some boiling water while trying to help Farah cook."

"Why the fuck am I just now hearing about it and where are you I hear machines?" She starts firing off questions while sliding her dress over her head and I'm grabbing my keys as well as my gun off the nightstand where I laid them earlier because I feel like I'm about to shot this stupid muthafucka.

"Farah thought it was minor when it happened but when I got home, he was still complaining about it and I noticed more redness than she said there should have been so we came to the ER for them to check it out but it's pretty bad. They are checking him now."

"You left my baby alone with this jealous bitch Darren." She screams as we are heading out the door to hop in my truck. We're in a rush so I just pick her up in place her in the seat and she smiles again then puts her seat belt on. I hop in myself and she is tearing into Darren.

"Darren, I don't want to hear that shit her and Kairo are completely different he's not jealous of you and you of all people should know the vindictive stupid shit a jealous person can do. What hospital are you at?" Once he tells her she hangs up in his face and that right leg starts to jump letting me know my angel is close to turning into a vicious mama bear.

"Baby let's just see what really happen before we jump to conclusions." I soothe her by rubbing the inner side of her thigh then squeezing slightly and she takes a deep breath as she turns to look at me.

"What would I do without you?" She ask as we pull up to the emergency entrance valet.

"You won't have to find out as long as I have a breath in my body." I declare giving her a quick kiss then handing the keys to the valet and walking to help her out. I almost clock that nigga over the head when I catch him eyeing her ass as he tries to hop in my truck. We get our visitor badges and head to where they moved him. We spot Darren having a hush conversation with Farah and then they spot us walking up. I don't like how their expressions changed.

"Y'all better move before I put y'all in a bed in this fuckin hospital." She sneers walking between them and a follow right behind her entering Zion's hospital room. They follow us in as she walks over to his side of the bed.

"The nurse gave him some ibuprofen for the pain after the doctor saw him." Darren informs her still standing by the door and I distract myself by texting my brother when she pulls the cover back to see where he's burned.

"My baby is in the fuckin burn unit with burns on his damn arm, parts of his chest, and leg. You must think I'm stupid to believe this was a God damn accident." She roars and fuck a bear my baby is a lioness about to pounce but I grab her up in my arms before she can reach the other side of the room.

"Baby I want to fuck them up to but Zion needs you. Look he's waking up." I whisper in her ear and she looks back to see the fear etched on his face when he looks from her to Farah and Darren. That shit just confirmed what I need to know and I am sure it did the same for her as well this shit was no damn accident.

"Aww mama's baby I'm here." He starts to cry and it shatters my heart when he tries to reach for her but winces in pain. Before either of us go off any further there is a knock at the door.

"Come in." I say while Lani tries to comfort Zion. I follow her as she walks on the other side of the bed where he's not burned so she can hold his hand while she squeezes mine.

"Good evening I'm Dr. Truman and you are?" The doctor introduces himself.

"I'm Dr. Arlani James his mother and this is my boyfriend Kairo. Doctor Truman how bad are my sons burns?" The doctor looks over to Darren and Farah who are now standing in the corner of the room looking like the cat that swallowed the canary.

"Well Dr. James to be frank *your* son has second degree burns on the right side of his body and with these type of injuries it is procedure to contact cps as they do not resemble accidental splash burns. In my professional experience they resemble burns that were made by a hot liquid being thrown at someone and that person turning to get away." The doctor explains and before I can stop her she launches herself across the room on Farah. Farah doesn't stand a chance against my angel. Lani has about three inches on her in height, probably a good forty or fifty pounds heavier, and my baby is throwing them haymakers. I wait a minute or two before I try to pull my baby off the dumb bitch and Darren doesn't even move to help her bitch ass off the floor. Dr. Truman is just standing there in pure shock and looks a bit satisfied too.

"I want this bitch arrested before I snap her fuckin neck and you." She shouts.

"Don't even think about it I want her ass up out of here just as much as you. I had my suspicions when I really looked at his burns but I'm no doctor and that's why we are here. The only reason I didn't say anything over the phone is so you didn't fly off the handles before it was confirmed." He reveals and I have a bit more respect for him now. Another knock comes at the door and in walks security along with what has to be a cps agent.

"CPS you aren't needed but it does look like we need an officer in here right away." Dr. Truman turns to tell them and the security guard gets on his walkie to have them send the resident officer up. Farah is still dazed and trying to get up from the floor thankfully so we don't have to worry about holding her ass down.

"Zi baby boy I am so sorry I put you in this position. I hope you can forgive me." Darren kneels beside his bed after kissing him on the forehead and I notice the tears streaming down his face.

"It's not your fault daddy. I should've told you she did it on purpose when you came home. You just seemed somewhat happy with her and the things she did before were just talking bad about mom and I told her to never do that again. Now that I think about it it's probably why she was mad."

"No baby boy this should have never happened at all. I love you so much." Darren says kissing his forehead again.

"He's right baby and thanks for taking up for mommy." She gives him a kiss next and he tries to move but winces in pain.

"I will order him something a bit stronger. That children's Tylenol didn't last long at all." Right as the doctor is about to leave the officer comes in to find Farah leaning up against the wall as she finally comes too. The doctor points to her and the officer walks in her direction.

"Her name is nmjjn Joseph officer and we want her charged with child abuse. How could you do this to my son Farah like I don't even understand this shit." He tells the officer. Watching Darren kneel back down by Zion's bedside, tears running down his face, I can't help but feel a pang of sympathy. Despite my anger, I see his pain and guilt, and for a moment, and I mean a moment, my heart softens. We're all hurting, and as much as I want to blame him, I know he's wrecked by this too. He's just a father desperate for forgiveness from his son at this point.

"Darren, *pleasssseee*, it was an accident, baby!" she cries out.

"This is all your fault, you smug, self-righteous bitch! All you had to do was stay in your damn place!"

Her begging turned to fury as soon as she sees Darren's cold indifference while the officer drags her away, kicking, screaming, and utterly humiliated. Moments later the door opens again with Mymy rushing in with Nasir and hurries to Arlani who has been connected to my side this whole time. The doctor leaves I assume to get Zi's pain meds put in.

"Aww Goddy baby. How the hell did this happen?" She looks back at us and Arlani explains everything we learned over the past hour or two. The nurse comes in to administer the pain meds the doctor ordered for Zion. He lasts about ten minutes before his eyes close, stay close, and then his light snores begin.

"I knew something was up with that bitch. Darren you need to pick better women the hell." Mymy fusses while kissing on Zion's face then standing upright and walking back to my brother's side.

"Baby have you eaten?" I question as I move her hair behind her ear.

"Dang I don't think I've eaten anything besides a sandwich I made when I got home earlier." She admits and I kiss her on the top of the head then whisper that I am going to grab us all something to eat. Nasir decides to ride with me and I smile at him giving Mymy a kiss before joining me out the room.

"Looks like you two have gotten cozy lil brother." I tease him while we walk down the hall. Nasir is a bit different emotionally then the rest of us. As a child a doctor told our parents he was on the spectrum, but they figured he just wanted an excuse to give him a pill and take him away to some special school. The man is deadly on a computer and just an all-around genius. We grab something simple for everyone since it's late and head back to the hospital. We all spend the night at the hospital since he has a private toom.

Chapter Nine

Arlani James

It's been couple weeks since my baby was burned by that insecure trifling bitch. He did his first week back to school from home since his burns weren't healing as quick as they should and that's when we found out his immune system was compromised. Today he's going to his father's house for the first time since Darren has been staying in the guest room to help take care of him and my man has been the biggest sweetheart. Kai and Darren have become close after realizing they have a lot in common with both of their father's being professors and the household dynamic that created for them. They even come from big tight knit families. Kai has transferred all his in-person clients to his gym manager and the rest of his trainers. He stays here most nights after handling his video clients since I don't have a home gym setup for him yet. Tonight, we are having dinner together at home and I am cooking his favorite shrimp alfredo with spinach and garlic bread. After getting the pasta boiling, I grab the bottle of white zinfandel out of the wine fridge, and I pour a much-needed glass. This past month or so has been one stressor after another and things are finally seeming to calm down. As I am draining the pasta Kai walks in the house and I smell his cologne before he even gets close.

"Hi, my angel you got it smelling real good up in here per usual." He says into my neck then gives me a kiss on my exposed shoulder since I am wearing one of the silk African patterned moomoo's he bought me, and it hangs off my shoulder a little. He leaves to wash his hands in the half bath down the hall then comes back and falls into groove with me cutting up the veggies while I clean the spinach. I pour him a glass of wine after I finish.

"Here's to a much-needed date night." I toast and he turns to clink his glass with mines then gives me a quick kiss on the lips. While the food simmers he grabs me in his arms to sway to the slow music I have playing.

"Hmm I'm about to say fuck this food and have you for dinner instead." He moans into my ear after twirling me around then pulling me back into to him.

"Don't tempt me with a good time." I shoot back. He releases me just enough to turn and cut the stove off. Before I can protest he has me thrown over his shoulder and is heading up the stairs to my room. He sits me on the edge of the bed gently then pulls my moomoo over my head and smiles at my glowing naked body. He pulls out his phone from his back pocket then presses the screen and I hear the alarm saying "Armed". I smile at the specimen of a man standing in front of me admiring every curve of his flexing muscles then his abs as he pulls his shirt over his head. I can't help myself, so

I lean forward to glide my tongue over his smooth dark chocolate skin and he just looks down at me with a smirk on his face. He's getting undressed too slow for me, so I decide to help him by leaning back then pulling down his sweatpants and the moment his thick, long dick is freed it pops up tapping me on my chin. I take that as a sign it wants to talk to my tonsils so I lean back so we can be eye to eye then slide my tongue around his head and then lean back just enough to spit on it. I use my tongue to spread it around then suck him into my mouth using my tongue to rub that thick under vein and grab his balls with one of my free hands to massage them as I move my head back then forward over and over again. I leave him as deep as I can take him and hum.

"Shiiittt that's my good lil slut. Suck you dick just like that." He groans then wraps my hair that's pulled into a ponytail around his hand then begins to fuck my mouth with a slow deep rhythm and I let him have his way. I create suction around his head when he starts doing quick and short thrust and I wrap my other hand as far it will go then start a squeeze twist motion.

"Hmmm fuck baby. You go bathe in this nut?" He groans so I suck harder then let his dick go and before I know it he's pulling his dick from mouth and shooting his cum all over my mouth, neck, as well as my exposed breast. I lick the cum around my lips and rub the remaining over my body then lick my hands clean.

"Fuck that was sexy as hell." He moans grabbing me by my neck then leaning down to give me a sloppy heated kiss tasting himself on my tongue and I can't help but moan myself.

"I see somebody is already soaked." He observes as he's rubbing his thick fingers through my slick lips then rubs some of my juices over my clit and I let out another moan. He removes his fingers from my pussy then wraps his tongue around his fingers like a snake sucking my juices from them. I can't help but bite down on my bottom lip and squirm as he's still holding me by my neck. He pushes me back on the bed then drops to his knees and grabs something from under the bed. When I notice it's the spreader bar he had delivered a few days ago I feel my juices rush from my pussy sliding down to my ass and dripping on the bed.

"Do you remember the video we watched. Are you ready for that baby?" He stands up holding my legs and looks me right in my eyes. We like to watch porn occasionally before or have it playing during sex, it fuels our kink a little of watching sex and the feel of someone watching us. I never thought it was something I was into until one night Mymy and Nasir walked in on us fucking on the couch and neither of us moved to stop or tell them to leave. I came so hard that night.

"Yes I remember." I answer finally coming back from that night.

"Good girl and safe word."

"Strawberry." I moan as he's fastening the straps around my ankles. I just had to be different and not just say red. He licks his lips as he tightens my right strap then pulls the bar as far as it goes a part and I cream again from pure anticipation of what he's going to do to me. He holds the center of the bar then kneels on the floor pushing the bar back towards my chest until my knees are touching my damn ears. He blows his cool breath on my clit that has already become sensitive so I can't help but squirm and he smacks me on either ass cheek.

"No moving or I will stop." He warns me after smacking me again and I can't help but bite down on my bottom lip. I still don't understand how he makes that shit hurt but feel good at the same damn time. He moans into my pussy as he licks up my juices that have slid down to my ass, dipping his tongue in my pussy then twirling his tongue around then finishing his way up to my clit and slurping on it like melting ice cream.

"Kaaaiii." I scream as he continues to slurp and flick his tongue against my clit. It takes so much control to keep from moving around under his touch from his hand that's roaming over my body and his tongue that's moving side to side over my clit. My body begins to tingle starting at my head, moving down my spine, I feel the tears streaming down my cheeks as the pressure builds between my legs and once it meets up with my tingles. I feel a gush of my juices sliding out of my pussy and Kai rushes to lick up every drop. The more he swirls his tongue in my pussy and sucks up my juices I cum even more so much, so I squirt all over his face.

"Shit I love it when you do that." He praises me as he stands up licking his lips then whipping his face with one hand and stroking his dick with the other. He walks over to my nightstand and pulls out my rose.

"Babe."

"Are you tapping out already my angel?" He questions as he walks over to me pressing the button on my rose.

"N...No." I answer with a slight stutter as he gets closer to me and grabs the bar.

"That's my lady." He praises me again then pushes the bar back again slowly entering me as he rests his knees on either side of me on the bed. He pushes so deep into me I swear it's like he's tapping my damn ovaries then he places the rose on my clit and I cum instantly.

"So responsive baby." He groans then he has the audacity to turn it up a level as he begins thrusting into me quicker.

"KAAAIIIII." I scream as I feel myself cum hard enough that I feel like I am having an outer body experience.

"That's it keep those juices flowing baby." He growls as he continues his assault on my pussy. He turns the rose up again but doesn't immediately place it back on my clit.

"Fu... Fuc... Fuccckkkk." I scream. Kai moves the rose, pulls the bar over his head so that he's between my legs, pushes his dick back up against my cervix and plants a heated kiss on my lips that takes my breath away. I can't help but to clench my walls around his hard length.

"You feel so good to me. I swear I could live in your pussy baby." He moans as he strokes me slowly but so deep. I realize he's giving me a slight break, but he feels just as good to me. His smooth skin rubbing against mines, our scents mingling together has become my favorite aphrodisiac, the flex of all his ripped muscles as he thrust into my tight pussy, and don't get me started on seeing his massive dick stretching me covered in my creamy juices. He bites down on my shoulder while he is still pumping into me with death strokes and I cum for like the fourth or fifth time tonight but this time I feel his dick twitch.

"Laniiii." He groans then growls in my ear as I start to feel his warm nut filling me up. We lay there for a moment trying to catch our breath then he slides from in between my legs and unfastens the straps around my legs. He picks me up then places me on the toilet while he gets my shower warmed up and this man proceeds to bathe me.

"Damn babe that feels amazing." I moan as he massages the shampoo into my scalp while I sit on the shower floor between his leg. We had to sit because my damn legs almost gave out. He insists on conditioning my hair even going as far as detangling then put my leave in conditioner and hair oil in my hair. I have never felt so pampered by a man in my life and I can definitely get use to this. While I am twisting my hair he's downstairs warming up our food since both of our stomachs are growling like a pack of ravenous wolves.

"Here you go baby." Kai hands me my plate on one of the bed trays I keep on hand.

"Thanks babe and thanks for going with water. I think you depleted me of all liquid's sir." I giggle taking a good sip of my water. We eat in a comfortable silence for a few minutes.

"Baby the day we had to rush to the hospital you were just about to tell me about your visitor. I'd be lying if I said I haven't been dying to know why she came to see."

"Kai-ro I never told you it was a she that popped up at the clinic." I turn my head to look at him and he drops his head telling me all I need to know. I can't help but laugh at my man's antics.

"You're not mad that I hacked your clinic cameras?"

"Before I would but I guess I understand your thought process more." He leans over to give me a quick kiss with a smile on his face.

"I would say I'd stop but baby whatever I have to do to make sure you and little Zi are good I will do it." He declares and you would think I'd be too tired or drained but my pussy just seriously clenched.

"I am ok with it babe. It really feels good having you be so protective over me but either way the chick that stopped by was the waitress from the restaurant I started telling you about."

"That's why she looked familiar."

"Yea she came to tell me about her and Chance. I knew it was something between them that night, but I never thought it was him pimping her out to his booky to repay his debt." I reveal.

"He did what to her?" He gasps.

"That's not even the whole story. They apparently met kinda like we did just out and about, but he had just loss big. He asked her out and they went out on a few dates before he popped up in her bedroom one night and when she woke up again she was some janky hotel room laying on the bed half dressed with Chance and a dude she figured was his booky from their arguments standing over the bed. They were arguing about him bringing an unconscious chick as his payment." I pause for a moment to finish off my water.

"Well, they went outside to figure out how many clients she would need to see before his debt was paid off and she found a way out the bathroom window. She didn't bother going to the police because she didn't think they would believe her story. She packed up and moved in with her sister then got hired at the restaurant hoping to never run into him again. So, when she saw him at the restaurant she was scared he would try to snatch her again or me for that matter. She looked me up and found out I was a doctor at the clinic she wanted to warn me." I finish telling him what she told me that day.

"I take it she doesn't know what exactly he wanted with you then." He grabs up our empty plates and stands to leave.

"No but the detective on the case left me a voicemail yesterday that they will have preliminary hearing in a few weeks since I confirmed I was pressing charges." I admit and look away because I know he's side eyeing me since he was asking me before what was going on with the case but I don't want him to find out he's out on bail. He puts down the trays and walks over to my new side of the bed since he's been practically living here.

"I know about the hearing and I also know that the piece of shit is out on bail but I promise I will not do anything crazy well unless they let him go then I have a few places for him to disappear to. But you ma'am for this to work out smoothly no hiding shit from me, understood?" He pins me with a stare that makes my pussy wet, but my mind obey.

"Yes I just don't want you to do anything crazy to get yourself put in jail. I love you." I pout and he gives me a slow sensual kiss.

"I love you too and it's why I promise to think before I act and occasionally run things by you before hand but I will forever protect my family and yes I said *My Family.*" He leans over to give me a quick kiss then leaves the room to put away the dirty dishes. I send a quick text to check in on Zion while my mind wonders on the possibility of Chance getting off and what might've happened had Kai not showed up that night.

Chapter Ten

Kairo Levi

It's time for this bitch ass niggas preliminary hearing and I am sitting in the back row with Nasir next to me. I made sure Arlani took her butt to work and I am here if they need a witness. She didn't need to hear none of this bullshit coming out his mouth right now. The prosecution had sufficient evidence and the defense rested without calling witnesses. I guess getting caught in the act along with being an asshole through text messages will do that. I have mixed feelings about them keeping him locked up until the trial unless he takes a plea deal which I am pretty sure they are going to offer him soon.

"Damn I was hoping they were going to release his ass. Those bullets you put in him weren't enough for me." Nasir groans as we walk out the court room.

"I feel the same way but wifey wants me on my best behavior." I say as we hop in my truck.

"Mymy said the same but that doesn't mean we can't touch him on the inside. He fucked with sis and that just can't slide." He declares with his infamous sneaky grin and I can't wait to see what this fool cooks up.

"Agreed." We dap and ride in silence for a bit. Tonight we are taking the ladies out for a movie then to dinner. They insisted on this darn black vampire movie which I'm fine with but they both know they are going to be scared. We get dressed at his condo since it's not far from our women plus do do brain didn't leave any clothes at my place and the both of them are still at work for a bit anyways. When we pull up to the house I can't believe the person standing outside banging on her door.

"Bro how the fuck did Kyla figure out where sis stay?" Nasir questions me and I am asking the same damn question. I pull up into the driveway and barely wait until I put the truck in park before I am throwing the door open.

"Kyla what the fuck are you doing here?" I ask as I snatch her off the porch by her arm.

"Kairo I am not just going to give up on us. I gave you some time come to your senses and did with that runt being in the hospital but now it's time you get it together and that heffa it's over." She sneers and it takes all my control to not knock her head off her shoulders. It's not like she's using it anyways. Before I can respond I see my woman pulling up next to my truck and I step back even further from delusional ass.

"Babe why is this bitch in front of my house?" I notice she left her purse and things in the car, well except for her car keys, which tells me one thing.

"I came to get my man so you can stop trying to guilt trip into to being with your fat ass." When my baby burst out laughing I know for sure her crazy has just been unlocked and all I do is step back. Nasir is just leaning against the truck chewing on that damn toothpick he always has when he's trying to calm his nerves. Before my angel pops off Mymy pulls up in her driveaway but by the time she's coming across the yard Lani has thrown a left hook and when she hits her with that right teeth come flying out of her mouth landing in front of Mymy.

"Ewww Kairo you mess with chicks with false teeth." Mymy screams kicking the teeth away from her and I can't help but bend over laughing. Kyla is laid out on the ground snoring and that just makes me laugh harder.

"Hey, she didn't have false teeth when we dated." I manage to get out while trying to catch my breath while still laughing. Lani smacks me on my arm as she's laughing her damn self. Nasir has cracked a smile and is shaking his head at us.

"Man, this dumb ass broad is going to make us late for our movie." Lani says as she is trying to stop laughing. We both notice at the same time Kyla starting to move around which is a good sign because she hit the concrete pretty hard and I'd hate for that to be on my baby conscious.

"Hmm looks like little dumb... dumb is waking up. I guess she thought because I'm doctor I wouldn't lay hands on her ass, ahh wrong. Come on wake up you are making us late." Lani finally stops laughing and kicks her leg.

"What the.. the hell? Kai bear you really let her hith me." She tries talking without her teeth she sounds like her tongues stuck to the top of her mouth and I can't help but laugh when she realizes her teeth are missing. This crazy broad sees them, picks them up, and puts them back in her mouth like it's nothing.

"Look I let sis handle you for a bit but I'm ready to hang with my fam so look here bitch stay the fuck away from my brother before I do worse than the nigga who made you need those. Now get yo coked head ass outta here." Nasir barks and I see the fear in her eyes when he mentioned the dude who made her need false teeth. She straightens her clothes then walks over to a car that was parked across the street and hops on the driver's seat then pulls off.

"Nasir." I call his name, and he already knows that we are about to have a fucking talk later. The girls go inside to get dressed and we make it just in time for the movie to start. As I thought they both screamed their heads off or hid in our arms most of the movie which turned out to be pretty good. We are waiting to be seated at my baby's favorite restaurant and thanks to setting reservations in advance we are seated pretty quickly.

"Babe I'll be back, you know what I like to drink." She announces then gives me a kiss on the cheek and walks over to the bathroom. The waitress comes and I order Lani's favorite wine and my top shelf whiskey. By the time Nasir and Mymy order their drinks and they are all brough back my angel is coming back but now she looks pissed off.

"What wrong baby?" I question her the moment she gets close.

"Is it piss Arlani off day or something? You won't believe who I just saw in the rest room." She huffs then falls into her seat.

"Hey, look at me what happen?" I question her again grabbing her by the chin because she has this spaced-out look and I have started to learn that my baby has a crazy side to her.

"That... That bitch Farah is here." She growls out low and I didn't even notice she picked up one of the steak knives on the table.

"Wait how the hell is she out of jail?" Mymy questions as she starts to stand when she zeros in on something. I follow her line of sight and spot Farah sitting at a table with an older gentleman and woman.

"Her father is some retired big-time judge. He was able to get her bail somehow, but I promise I will find out how sis and expose them both. She won't get away with hurting my nephew." Nasir fills us in.

"So, you really can find out anything Nasir, well when you find it I want you to ruin them. You are so right nobody hurts my baby." She declares and he nods his head. We eat in peace until the dumb bitch decides to walk over to our table.

"You better walk the fuck off before jail time is the least of your worries." Mymy scoffs as she stands from her seat, but Nasir grabs her hand to keep her from jumping on this dumb ass chick. Luckily Lani is sitting to my left, and I am sitting near the aisle otherwise she'd already be on her ass.

"Look just drop the charges, we can forget this ever happened, and you can have them both for all I care." Farah advises and something about the way she says it makes me feel like there is an underlined threat in there.

"I'm not dropping shit. You will be punished for what you did to my baby one way or the other you pathetic, sour pussy, French poodle looking bitch. Let me go Kai." She fights to get around me but there is no way in hell I am letting her go with all these people around and she's holding that damn steak knife again.

"No baby don't give her the satisfaction. We will handle this shit I promise you that." I stand fully in her view then grab her face with both hands to make her look me in the eyes and she begins to calm down. I take the knife from her and then I notice the man that she was sitting with walk towards our table.

"Farah I told you not to come over here. She's not ready to talk to you babygirl." The man says to her then grabs her by the arm.

"Of course, she's not ready to speak to the woman who burned her son with hot water *on purpose* just because her jealous and insecure ass couldn't comprehend English." I spit out and he looks like this is news to him.

"Oh, wait let me guess she told you it was an accident; well, it wasn't your precious daughter is a child abuser." Nasir says next while I comfort more like continue to calm my angel who is shaking and crying she's so mad.

"My daughter would never purposely hurt a child she works with them every day." He announces. I look at Nasir and he's already on his phone typing away. I can always count on him to handle business.

"Well, she hurt mines. She will pay for it and it's nothing you can do about it either." Lani looks around me and promises the judge. He finally pulls a frowning

Farah away from our table and when I look back at Nasir he has a satisfied smile on his face.

"Let's go, my appetite is ruined." Lani announces.

"Nasir take the ladies outside I will get the bill." He nods then stands pulling out Mymy's chair as I do the same for my angel then give her a kiss on the forehead before Nasir takes her hand as well to walk them outside. I call the waitress over for the bill and to go boxes. When she comes back the older woman that was sitting with Farah walks over and I hope she has more sense because I'd hate to cuss an old lady out today.

"Hi, I just wanted to apologize for my daughter and husbands' interruption earlier. I did want to ask you something however." I turn to give her my attention.

"Did my daughter really hurt her child? Like do you know that for sure?" She questions me and I can tell she genuinely wants to know.

"Yes your daughter threw boiling hot water on my stepson giving him second degree burns all because she is jealous of my woman and the co-parenting relationship she has with her son's father." She gasps and puts her hands over her mouth. I see tears start to well up in her eyes as it all sinks in.

"Oh, my goodness, I am so sorry. I've been telling my husband she needs help again. Once again I am so sorry." She apologizes then walks off to the exit. While we were speaking the waitress packed up our food and came back with my card. I leave her a tip and walk off to meet the fam at my truck with Farah's mothers words replaying in my mind. We all decide to stay at my house and the girls are in the back putting on something comfortable.

"So, nigga how did you know about what happened to Kyla's trifling ass. Well, I take that back I'm sure I can guess how but why and what else do you know?" I ask him as I sip on some of the wine we pulled out.

"So, after I found out she was cheating on you. I had some friends follow her for a few days and whoever the nigga she was cheating with dropped her off to another dude at some shady hotel. When I checked back into her after she popped up at the event I discovered she became an escort but apparently she got out of line at some point, and he beat her up pretty bad. Part of me thinks she gets she fucked up and that's why she's back, but the other side thinks that sneaky bitch is up to something." He explains and now I am in my head trying to figure out what the hell she may be up to so I can end this shit. Before we go any further the girls come back dressed in the moo moos I bought Lani and put in the closet.

"So, what are we doing?" Mymy questions as she sits on Nasir's lap in the chair across from me. Lani goes to sit on the arm of the chair, but I grab her to sit on my lap.

"I have something to tell you sis." Nasir says as he plays in Mymy's wild afro. Lani nods for him to continue.

"So, I looked further into Farah and her parent's. Farah works for a private school as a teacher's aide and she has been committed to the crazy house more than once. This Is not the first time her father has tried to cover up something bad she has done. Oh, Darren is not the first dude she's dated with a child and something crazy happened to said child or the child's mother. So no more going out on your own for awhile Lani. Brother do you want me to call my security friends?" She squirms in my lap, and I see the look on her face like she's not having it.

"No, I will close my schedule for the next few weeks but have them continue to dig into her and that father I am sure it's something we can use to get her bail revoked and you ma'am don't give me any push back. I will be with you everyday until both these crazy fucks are dealt with, understand?" I turn her head to look at me and she has the audacity to pout but then nods her head to agree.

"Well as long as it's you following me around all day and as long as we can get in some quickie time in throughout the day." I bite down on her shoulder then she closes her eyes and moans.

"We can do as many quickies as you like my angel." I groan into her ear while doing circles on her inner thigh. She spreads her legs a little and I take that as a hint to slide my hand up to her pussy that's already wet for me. I rub my fingers around in her juices then slide my finger to her clit and apply pressure while rubbing circles.

"Kaiii." She moans without a care that my brother and her bestfriend are right across from us. They are wrapped up in their own sexual activity. Nasir has Mymy moo moo pulled up with her straddling him.

"Hmmm this pussy is always so wet and ready for me. Look you've turned them on too." I turn her head towards Mymy and Nasir and Mymy is either riding his fingers, or he's pulled out his dick but she's rocking her hips. I lift her up then turn her to face them while still on my lap and lift her again to pull her dress up then settle her back in my lap but with her back against my chest legs spread wide. Let's see how far this goes tonight.

Chapter Eleven

Arlani James

I can't believe this man has me spread eagle on his lap while his large fingers are sliding in and out of my wet pussy, he licks and sucks on that sensitive spot on my neck, all in front of my best friend and his brother. Nasir has turned Mymy around on his lap and she's now riding him reverse cowgirl.

"You like this don't you Angel?" Kai groans into my ear as he slides his fingers from pussy.

"Ye… Yes." I moan as I wind my hips over his hard length attempting to get some friction since he's stopped fingering me. He grabs my dress and starts pulling it over my head. I hesitate for a moment not knowing how I feel about being naked in front of his brother, Mymy has seen me naked before hell we even tried the whole lesbian thing back in college when we swore off dudes for a semester but I decide quickly to let him. I have been wanting to experience the whole voyeurism and exhibitionism thing in person the videos have not been enough lately. He starts rubbing circles around my right nipple then pinches and twist.

"Put your legs on the arm of the chair." He commands and I do exactly as he says. I notice Mymy and Nasir watching me while she grinds on his dick that has her pussy stretched. I have a full view since he's spread her legs and long ago removed her dress. Kai makes a movement, and Nasir nods his head when Mymy looks back at him. She stops riding his dick, he releases her legs, then she gets up and crawls over to us. Kai lifts me up then slowly lowers me down on his hard dick and my breath gets caught in my throat.

"Breathe baby." He commands as he drops me the last inch.

"Fuckkk." I moan. Mymy just made it over to us and she sits kneeled with Nasir right behind her. He whispers something in her ear and she gets this sly one-sided smile. She scoots closer to me at the same time Kai slumps a little in the chair then starts pumping into me and when she licks from where his dick s stretching me like panty hoses four times to damn smile up to my clit I get even wetter than I already was. My eyes roll in the back of my head as she latches on to my clit with her soft lips and Kai continues thrusting in and out of me.

"Open those pretty eyes baby. I want you to see all the nasty shit that juicy pussy causes." My eyes shoot open when Mymy moans as she's sucking and flicking her tongue across my clit. I look down at Kai's dick coated in my juices and clench my walls tight. My nut hits me like a head on car collision when I realize Mymy is riding Nasir's face while she's nose deep in my pussy.

"Ooooh shit... shit. Don't stop please." I moan. I swear these two have found a damn rhythm because at his next thrust in and her side lick of her tongue I am cumming again and this time I squirt.

"Unt uh don't move." He demands grabbing the back of her head pressing it firm into my pussy as I continue to cum. My nut last so long I can't help but close my eyes and the moment I do Kai takes one of his hands to wrap around my neck then thrust harder.

"Didn't I say keep those eyes open." He groans. Mymy takes one more lick over his dick to my clit then moans out her own release.

"Fuck Nas... Shhhiiittt." She screams as he continues to eat her pussy through her orgasm. He stops after another minute or two then slides from under but quickly turns around pushes her forward by the back of her neck and I get a glimpse of his large chocolate dick pushing into her quick and to the hilt.

"Fuck baby." She moans.

"You like this don't you baby." I can't do anything but nod my head as Mymy has sucked my clit back into her warm mouth as Nasir fucks her hard from the back. A whimper leaves my throat as I cum again. Nasir snatches Mymy back and tongue kisses her then moans as he tastes my juices on her tongue. This time I see when Kai signals for them to move back and when they do he stands still holding but plants me on my feet.

"Lay down on your back baby." Kai instructs me. These two proceed to have Mymy and I lay in the sixty-nine position with them fuckin us into orgasmic bliss. I am completely jelly at this point.

"Come on baby let me get you cleaned up. Y'all know where the guest rooms are." He says picking me up bridal style off the floor and heads to his master bedroom. He proceeds to clean me thoroughly I may add then makes me a snack and before you know it I am out like a light.

Chapter Twelve

Kairo Levi

"You know I'm going to finish this once and for all right." I say to Nasir as we stand in the kitchen sipping on my favorite Whiskey.

"And you know I'm ridin with you big bro. So, what we doing?" He responds like I knew he would, so I push the hidden button on the side of the island and out pops two racks of weapons. He catches my drift then walks over to the pantry and opens the hidden door to reveal more weapons as well as armor. Our father might've been a knowledge led man but he always knew life wouldn't be fair for us as black men or women no matter the time we lived in so we had to know how to protect ourselves and the families we all would one day have. I am expert marksmen and trained by ex-military in hand-to-hand combat and so is Nasir, hell he's the only one of us besides me that mastered Tae and Jiu Jitsu. Once we get everything we need setup I go back into my room to look at my sleeping angel.

"Baby I promise I've thought this through, but I have to release you from this bullshit once and for all. I wouldn't be the man I told you I would be if I didn't. Please don't be too mad when you wake up, I love you my angel." I kiss her softly on her lips and she stirs just a little bit. I head out the room and spot Nasir walking out of the guestroom he's sharing with Mymy, and he has his head down.

"Hey, pick yo head up. We will make it back home to them." I declare and pat him on the shoulder. He picks his head up smiling and I realize this fool was praying for our enemies again. I just shake my head at his crazy ass. He likes to say that is the only way they will get mercy from him only if God himself grants it. We grab our backpacks and hop on our motorcycles we keep in the second garage, and we head to our destination on the other side of town with blood on our mind. When we reach about five minutes from the new hotel they are working out of we park our bikes in the alley.

"Aight according to my contacts he keeps two guards with him plus his driver. They are on the second floor in the back and the girls are always in the joining room but from what he just sent me they are all out." He gives me the run down and we come up with a plan of attack. We decide to split up and he takes out the driver while I get up the stairs and take the one that stands at the door and catch his big ass before hits the floor. Nasir meets me by the door the girls are usually in, and he unlocks the door with a master keycard. Thankfully the door doesn't make too much noise, but they probably wouldn't hear it over the music they have playing now. When we enter the room Nasir takes out his last guard while catching Kyla's pimp right in his hip bone causing him to hit the floor in pain. Thanks to our silencers and the fact that they thought it was a good idea to have the room at the end of the hall we could careless about anyone possibly hearing us but I turn the music up a little more anyways.

"Hey, wait fuckin minute isn't this Chance's bookie?" I ask Nasir as he puts him in a chair in the corner of the room and I throw him the rope.

"You know what it is. I mean he's a bit more on the Michelin tire man side than the pic that was sent with his file but hell yea." He answers as he ties him up.

"Look what do y'all want? I have money, you can have it. I have girls with some of the best pussy in town they can be back here in minutes." He says desperately to let him go and crying in pain.

"Is this really the nigga that knocked Kyla's teeth out, can't be." I look over at Nasir while pulling one of my blades from my boot.

"Wait this is about Kyla? Look you can have her ass she's too coked out now anyways." He tries barging with us and this nigga must be stupid if he thinks I'd do all this over her bum ass.

"It's about Kyla, Chance and why the fuck you have them messing with my fuckin family." I growl jabbing my blade into his thigh purposely missing anything vital. Moms taught us a lot about the body as well. I can probably do this for hours before hitting any major organs. He goes to scream when I snatch the blade out, but Nasir is quick to cover his mouth with a towel to muffle him.

"Start talking before it gets a lot worse for you. I may even decide to let you live with all limbs if you give me everything I need to know." I bargain with him and look up at Nasir. I can clearly read on his face that I may but he for sure will not and I can't help but chuckle inward.

"What do you want to know, man that shit hurt." He groans and shakes his head because the pain from both wounds is starting to get to him.

"Why the fuck is Kyla been on my ass so heavy and what does she have to do with Chance?" I question sitting backwards in the chair facing him.

"Look Kyla use to be Chance's bitch a few years ago after he took her from some personal trainer lame and when he couldn't pay his debt he dropped her off to me but never came back for her. It became a thing with him. When he gambles and loses too much he pays with some chick dumb enough to like his broke ass." He takes a deep breath and winces in pain when he moves in his seat then his face goes white when I pull my mask down so he can see my face.

"Yea the lame now continue before my patience runs out." I threaten him through gritted teeth.

"Look I didn't mean nothin by it, but I sent Kyla to you because like I said she's no use to me now that she is sloppy hooked and trying whatever she can get her hands on. I told her dumb ass to go back to you because you clearly had more money than she thought to pay the debt she now owes. Well, you know how that has been playing out and same thing with Chance and this doctor bit-" I jab my blade in his other thigh before he gets the word fully out his mouth. I don't know why niggas think it's ok to talk crazy about my woman like that.

"Fuccckkk." He groans as his scream is muffled by Nasir again.

"Watch ya mouth about that one if you want to live, understand?" He nods his head and Nasir releases him.

"Look I didn't know she was ya girl too. Chance seems to have a hard on for your women. I mean look look." He pleads as I have the blade in the air about to stab his slick mouth ass again.

"He owed me again and offered her up but this time it was shit it was getting what we need for our drugs from her clinic but then I heard that nigga was shot and now I can guess by who. Damn did you have to kill them both? It's hard to find good help these days." He groans looking around at both his dead guards and we both shrug out shoulders.

"You got the message I wanted by killing them didn't you?" He nods then lowers his head.

"Well, you wrap ya wounds up and get to a doctor soon you should be good but one more thing do you know a Farah?" When I ask about her he throws his head back and starts crying.

"Just kill me dammit I'm not talking about that psychotic bitch ever again." I can only imagine what caused that reaction.

"Are you sure because that can be arranged and I promise it won't be quick." I warn him tilting my head to side turning the knife in my hand. He heeds my warning.

"Look she's the judge's daughter and if you mess with her you will find yourself in prison or come up missing. He doesn't care if it's something she did wrong so if you've found yourself in her crosshairs good luck and that's all I'm saying." He groans in pain, and I stand to leave.

"Well, you've served your purpose and as I promised you are free to go." Nasir grunts behind him and that lets me know he's killing his ass so how is the only question. I nod my head, leave the room then lean against the rail and light my joint. We both smoke but it's really rare that we do but tonight really calls for it because if what he says is true this judge is about to be a serious fucking problem. I use my burner to hit up one of my contacts while this nigga still in there torturing dude. I send an email to the family lawyer to contact some of his judge friends to see just what we may be in store for. After about thirty minutes Nasir comes out and I'm sure if he wasn't wearing all black I would see that he's covered in blood.

"I already called the clean up crew but it's nothing left of us in there anyways." He announces taking off his gloves then pushing them in his pockets. When we start walking downstairs our normal cleanup crew is coming up stairs. We fist bump each of them and keep walking. Some may ask why we even have one on speed dial, but we occasionally do some crazy shit and need it to be handled quickly. Our clean-up crew consists of our college friend's crime scene cleaning company and some of the dudes from their old hood. We hop on our bikes then stop by his condo to get cleaned up before heading back to our women. Walking in the door the house is still pitch dark but then the flick on before we even make it through the living room. When our eyes adjust to the light we notice our women sitting on the couch, legs and arms crossed, hair still wrapped in their silk scarfs, and faces twisted up.

"So, where the fuck were you two?" Arlani says first with her head tilted to the side.

"We had to go handle some business." I answer.

"What fuckin business could the two of you be handling at two in the morning?" Myasia sneers.

"We betta tell em." Nasir looks at me and I just nod my head in response. We sit with them and fill them in on what we did as well as what we discovered. Nasir thankfully holds back the details of how he tortured buddy but that didn't seem to calm the frustrations in the ladies.

"Yall could've been shot. What the fuck were you two thinking?" My angel is clearly worried as she smacks me on the arm. I stand up bending over to grab her and walk off to my bedroom. Once we get behind the door I kick it close with my foot then lay her on the bed.

"Baby look at me. I am here and I am in the same condition I left in." I assure her then place her hand on my chest.

"Take off your clothes." She orders me and I don't waste time thinking about it. I stand from leaning over her taking off my shirt the moment I'm up right then drop my basketball shorts and stepping out of them revealing my naked lower half since I went with no boxers. She stands and actually inspects my front and back for any marks.

"Feel better now baby?"

"You bathed." She says more as a discovery not a question.

"Yes baby I had blood on me, and I had to burn my clothes." I explain as she's rubbing her hand down my torso then wraps her beautiful, manicured hand around my dick and I bite down on my bottom lip.

"You didn't have enough of me earlier baby?" I moan out as she begins stroking my dick with her soft hands.

"I will never get enough of you. As scared as I was after what you guys told us I was also turned on to be reminded just how much you love and will do to protect me. I will just be more at peace when you won't have to go through such extremes to do so. I love you Kairo." She expresses her feelings then lays her head on my chest while still stroking my dick. I lift her head and gently kiss her soft lips. Before we can get any sleep I have her ass up in the air and her face pushed into the pillows with me in a squat position fuckin her so deep she feels me tapping on her ovaries. We get cleaned up then finally lay down to get some sleep.

Chapter Thirteen

Arlani James

It's been a crazy week since Kai and Nasir dealt with Chance's bookie and apparently Kyla's pimp. Let's not forget Farah was somehow connected to his ass. What's been making crazy is the fact that her father has had people following me and trying to intimidate Darren into dropping charges against her. Kai has been on one with them though, he has hired lawyers, private investigators, and given Darren information on the security team they usually use. As Kai promised me he has been by my side at work, he picks up Zion occasionally then brings him to the clinic when I've worked late and today is one of those days. The clinic has picked up the flow of patients since hiring the other doctors, the healthcare even some of us attended last month, and my assistant's constant bagger to up our social media presence. Today it's just me and one other doctor taking care of the last few patients and Kai is gone to drop Zion to Darren's since they are leaving for the weekend to visit his parents in Florida for their fortieth anniversary.

"Alright Mrs. Julien everything is looking good with your levels, that new diet has been working for you." I say then notice I hear a commotion in the hall and a loud boom. I grab for my phone in my pocket but before I can view the camera's or call Kai the exam room door fly's open and in walks two large men with mask on. They don't even say anything they just lunge towards me, but I am able to evade them at first. I'm able to press call on Kai's name as I make it around the exam table.

"KAAAIII." I scream the moment the call connects and one of them snatches me up since I have nowhere else to run plus the other has Mrs. Julien by the neck threatening to hurt her. I can't let them hurt her so I stop fighting and the other man throws her to the floor then they rush towards the back door by my office. I hear sirens faintly in the distance as they run then throw me in the trunk of a car. They clearly have to be amateurs the dummies didn't bother to take my phone or my watch in their haste to get me out of my office. The car pulls off with a jerk and then it starts speeding down the road. I hear muffled shouts from inside the car but I can't really make out what they are saying. The smell of strong cleaning and metal smell in the trunk is irritating the hell out of my nose causing me to have a sneezing fit.

"Lani, Lani baby can you hear me?" I hear Kai come through on my phone that I forgot I still had on me.

"Yes... Yes, babe I hear you. Please come and get me. I'm scared." I whisper as the realization that I have really been kidnapped sinks in.

"I'm coming for you baby I promise. I am tracking you as we speak. Don't worry Zion is safe with Darren and their security team." He assures me but panic sinks in further as the car feels like it's slowing down.

"Babe how are you going find me if they take my phone? I think we're stopping." I question him as worry and fear settle in my chest.

"Touch your necklace or your bracelet. Baby I am always with you. Now stay quiet and take some deep breaths I'm coming for you." He reassures me. I don't even trip out that this crazy man has put tracking devices in the gold amethyst set he bought me about two months ago. I put the phone up under my thigh then take my watch off and put it in my coat pocket. The car comes to a complete stop then I hear both car doors open.

"How could you forget to check her or take her damn phone you fucking idiot." One of the men shouts as they walk around the car and their voices become louder.

"Look I'm not going to be too many of your fucking idiots. We were in a rush nigga." The other man shouts back as I hear them open the trunk. The sun blinds me for a moment, and I can't make out either of them,

"I mean she does look good if boss decides not to return her I will gladly keep her." The larger of the two men says and I scoot back but I bump into something sharp that jabs me in the back.

"This is why I don't like doing shit with yo weirdo ass now. I'll check her instead." The shorter man groans then leans over to start patting me down. He takes my watch then pushes me over trying to check my other pockets and discovers my phone.

"Look behave and do what the boss ask, and you will be back taking care of patients and your kid before you know it." He warns me in a tone that tells me he would rather be doing anything else but this right now. The creepy one leans over and picks something up that I soon find out is duct tape. He rips a piece with his teeth then places it over my mouth and gets mad when I move my head away from him when he goes to rub my cheek. He goes to hit me, but the other guy stops him then pushes him back and slams the trunk. We've been driving now for a while, and I really hope Kai is still able to track me. We come to a stop finally and dammit I am glad because it's hot as hell in this fuckin trunk.

"Aight come now and don't cause no trouble." The nicer of the two warns me again after pulling the duct tape off my mouth then he reaches to pull me out the trunk. A black bag is quickly thrown over my head, but I catch a glimpse of a large Victorian house surrounded by trees. They drag me along this smooth walkway then we switch over to grass and I hear a heavy squeaky door open.

"Step down." The creep orders and I realize then that we are descending downstairs possibly into a basement or cellar. When we get to the bottom I am pushed down into a chair.

"Tie her to the chair." I hear a different voice order the two men to do then I feel what must be rope wrap around my wrist that are pulled behind me. I hear another chair scrape across the hard floor then stop right in front of me.

"No leave that on. All I have to say is drop the charges on Farah Joseph and you can go back to your little clinic."

"Fuck you I am not dropping shit on the pathetic child abusing funky coochie bitch. She lucky-" A large hand comes across my cheek causing my ear to ring.

"Don't you dare talk about m... about her that way. She would never hurt a child on purpose. You're just jealous of her."

"Pshh jealous of her for what. I help people not hurt them, I've built my wealth on my own, and if a man doesn't want me I know how to move the fuck on." I put emphasizes on that last part because this insecure bitch is the only reason I am in this damn situation.

"Bitch you have one more time to speak ill of her."

"Aw *Judge* did I strike a nerve talking about your psychotic daughter."

"What the fuck I thought you said she couldn't see through that thing." I hear him jump up from the chair and it falls over as he's in a panic.

"Yes I know who you are and no I can't see you so thanks for confirming what your voice already told me." I sneer then I hear a loud commotion.

"You idiots did someone follow you here?" He questions them.

"Hey, get the boss out of here I'll deal with her and our intruders." The nicer of my kidnappers instructs the other.

"No, I want you with me he can kill her ass and deal with whoever thought it was a good idea to come for her." My heart stops when he says that but knowing my man has showed up for me yet again it starts up again. I hear gunfire ringing off upstairs then a door bust opens to my left at the same time I hear the heavy doors we entered in open. Before I can scream for Kai something heavy hits me across the head and everything goes completely black.

Chapter Fourteen

Kairo Levi

I still can't believe this muthafucka had the nerve to take my woman broad fuckin daylight from her clinic. I calmed her down as much as I could in the short time I could speak to her then immediately got on the phone with my brother.

"Nas they took her they fuckin took Arlani! Meet me at the house." I shout the moment he answers the call, and he doesn't bother with unnecessary words he just ends the call. When I reach the house I notice him and two other vehicles pulling up with and I don't have to guess who they are because the moment they come to a stop our cousins, eight in total are hoping out of them. None of us even speak we just nod our heads then walk into the house gearing up for whatever was necessary to bring my girl home. Mymy sat balled up on the couch crying as she was with Nas when I called him. I nudge him since he's standing next to me packing his bag and I nod my head towards her when he looks up at me. He still occasionally needs reminders of his emotional priorities; he gets hyper focused on whatever he's doing and nothing else matters. He comforts her while I finish packing both our bags then head for the door.

"Kai I know you love her but that's my other half I don't know a life without her she's more than my bestfriend she...she's-" She stutters tearing up again.

"Mymy don't worry I will bring her back." I assure her and lean over the couch to give her a one-armed hug. Nas gives her a kiss then we all pile up in two trucks and head to where they are holding my girl. I call my cousin in the other truck and put it on the speaker.

"Yo." He answers.

"Aight look they have her about and 30 minutes away in some old ass neighborhood. From the records I pulled most of the homes are either abandoned or owned by some corporation and a few old folks." I fill them in on what I'm finding out as I pull up information on Nas's laptop since he's driving.

"Ok so we don't have to worry about any eyes on us. How did you even find her so quick?" One of them asks.

"That's my soon to be wife nigga I never lost her. She has more than one tracking device on her at all fuckin times." I answer full of confidence.

"Dis nigga was always a lil off." One of them say from the backseat and I turn to look at him with a smirk on my face.

"Kai you do know that's not normal, right?"

"Normal or not she loves every bit of it nigga." We make it there but park about four houses down.

"Hey, we buying this block." My cousin Juice states hopping out the back of the truck and looking around at all the old homes. That nigga is always ready to buy up some real estate and he knows I'm with him every time. Nas sends up the drone as Juice walks up to the house of the old couple drive through we parked in then hands the old man a stack of money the moment he opens the door. He nods his head over to our trucks and the old black man smiles then put his hand out for Juice to shake which he obliges.

"Hey, he has about four niggas in there and according to these blueprints it's a basement and since I don't see any signs of Lani upstairs I can only assume she's one of the heat signatures in the basement." Nas explains as he's bringing the drone back in. We come up with a plan and half of us go to the back then the rest go to the front. We went with rubber rounds just in case the police show up and we start letting them off the moment we enter the house. One of the guards tries to run to the basement but Nas hits him with a rubber bullet right to the center of his forehead and we see the knot forming as we walk in his direction. When I step to the door this big nigga starts shooting but before I duck behind the wall I notice my angel laying on the ground and two niggas running out a side door.

"Yo go get catch those niggas that went out the side of the house." I order. Juice and two of our cousins rush out the back door. The nigga downstairs is still shooting well until Nas gets down on the floor and send off a few shots himself after switching his gun with regular bullets. When I hear hid body hit the floor I make my way downstairs checking to see if anyone is hiding with Nas on my heels while the others sweep the house.

"Shit baby I got you." I take the bag off her head then move her plaits from her face and slowly check her for any other injuries besides the gash on her forehead that's clearly from the butt of a gun striking her. I don't see any other wounds besides the handprint on the other side of her cheek that I know can only be by that bitch ass judge.

"You think it's a good idea to move her Kai?" Nasir asks me as I go to lift her up and I hesitate for a minute then check her again. I decide to play it safe and call for an ambulance. I have my cousins dip all but Juice listens. When the police and ambulance make it they handcuff us while they look over the scene, calling another ambulance for the nigga Nas shot and call me shock when the old man comes down the street telling the officers to let us go. He started complaining about the strange things he's seen or heard coming from the house. I had the woman officer who recognized me from my videos take my lawyers card from my pocket because we had nothing to say. Lani still hadn't regained consciousness by the time they drove away and all I want to do is get to her. After about forty-five minutes of them going back and forth they finally let us go after setting up for us to come in with our lawyer tomorrow morning. We walked off with the old man back to his home and sure enough none of these fools actually left they just posted up at his home. I walk into his home, and I am instantly hit by that old house smell, but I can also smell the mold in the air.

"I know your cousins have already told me young man. They even offered to have everything fixed but I can't possibly pay them back for everything they want to do even with the money they gave me." He explains as he slowly lowers his small frame into a black weathered looking recliner. I see the look in Juice's eye then follow his line of sight to the medals on the wall.

"Mr?"

"Just call me Jimmy son."

"Jimmy you served a country that could care less about you clearly the least we can do is give you a comfortable home to live out your golden years especially after what you did for us." I tell him as I squat down and place my hand on his shoulder. He starts to tear up but turns his head.

"He's right old head we gotcha. No payback needed. I've already made some calls to my construction office to put a team together that will start tomorrow morning." Juice says from his other side with finality in his tone.

"I just put you on my grocery delivery list too and no arguing you coming with us tonight." Nasir says coming from exploring the old man's home.

"I... I really don't know what to say. God really has way showing out doesn't he. I literally just sent my wife of thirty years away because this house was slowly killing her to live with her sister. It has been killing me to think I was going to really leave the home I grew up in behind. You fellas won't change too much of it will ya?"

"Jimmy we are just paying for it you and your wife are designing it. We can tell this place means a lot to you." Juice explains to him, and I know he's seeing his dad in the old head. He's always been soft towards vets because of Unc but after he passed away a few years back it's been even more. We pack him up with a few things then head out. The fellas drop Nas and me at the hospital while they take him to get settled in one of our rental properties. He called his wife while we were driving, and she was jumping for joy. She even said a prayer for my angel had us all in the truck crying. It's something about those old school prayer warrior mamas that just hit ya soul every time. We get checked in then head up to her room the moment I get settled next to her in the chair a crying Mymy comes rushing in. She rushes to her side rubbing her bandage head.

"Thank you so much Kai you too baby for bringing my girl back to me." She leans over her giving me as tight of a hug as she can then give Nasir a slow kiss holding both sides of his face and I can feel the heat rolling off those two from here.

"Ight you two can get a room." I say with a smirk and Mymy turns to stick her tongue out at me. I start laughing but stop immediately when I hear my baby's voice so low I almost missed it.

"Aww baby don't move. I will call for the doctor." I coach her to lay back down as she was trying to sit up and looks around confused. Mymy presses the call button for the doctor, but it takes a few minutes for the nurse to come in and let us know he will be in shortly after checking her vitals. The doctor checks her out and determines the hit to her head was hard enough to possibly cause a concussion, but they will verify with some test. She informs us that the tech will be in as soon as they can because the hospital is quite busy tonight.

"I knew you would come for me babe. I wasn't scared at all, pissed but not scared." She expresses and I lean over to give her a kiss.

"As long as my limbs still have movement and heart beats I'm coming for you Arlani." I give her another kiss on the lips this time as a knock comes at the door then it opens.

"Arlani James?" A badly dressed middle aged black man calls out after entering the room with a older white just as badly dressed man.

"Who are you two?" I question as I stand while still holding my angels hand.

"I am detective Hunter, and this is my partner detective Perkins we have a few questions for Ms. James." The black one introduces them. I pull out my phone and call my lawyer then I notice Mymy pull out her phone, but she just sits it face down next to Lani. When my lawyer answers I tell him what's happening then I put him on the speaker.

"Ok go ahead."

"Well Ms. James can you tell us what happened today?" She goes on to explain everything from the doctor's office to being tied up in that house in the basement. When she mentions the judge the other decides to talk.

"That can't be possible Judge Joseph is a very respectable man he has no need to kidnap someone." Detective Perkins gets on the defense.

"I know his voice he ran up on me in a restaurant because his bat shit crazy daughter abused my child." She shoots back looking at him sideways.

"What makes you think it was Judge Joseph besides a simple voice you heard?" I'm getting irritated with the line of question already, but I will let my woman handle herself and jump in when needed. She goes on to tell them about the charges on his daughter and him asking her to drop them.

"Look we are going to do our jobs and find who kidnapped you but ma'am I can guarantee you it wasn't him." He declares closing his notepad then dropping his pen in the pocket of his wrinkled button up shirt.

"You will do your job and explore every avenue including the Judge. I will be on a conference call with Deputy Sheriff Truman and Chief Brand in thirty minutes. Kairo I will call you later with any updates." Our lawyer declares and ends the call. The white officer fidgets with his crooked tie then runs his hand over the wrinkles in his shirt clearly bother by who was just mentioned.

"Ms. James we have your clothes for evidence and if it's ok we will have the csi tech come in to take pictures of your wounds." Detective Hunter states.

"As long as he stays I am fine with that." She responds looking up at me. It wasn't any chance I was leaving any damn way.

"Well let us go Nas baby and get her some clothes from the house. I'm sure you guys are all hungry too." Mymy says picking up her phone while kissing Arlani on the cheek. Once those two leave so do the detectives but they send in the techs to do their jobs which thankfully didn't take that long because soon the hospital tech came in to take her for cat scan while she was out doing that I walked down the hall for some of their nasty hospital coffee.

"I don't give a shit what that black bitch says Judge Joseph is a stand-up guy and will be helping me finally get out of this dead position. She probably was fuckin around and didn't want to get caught by her big ass boyfriend in there, so we are burying this that's final." I hear detective Perkins does a bad job at trying to whisper to detective Hunter around the corner from the coffee section. I want to walk around and put his bitch ass in one of these hospital beds, but detective Hunter starts talking.

"We will do no such thing. There are witnesses at her clinic that proves two men snatched her from there and threw her in the trunk of a car. On top of that whoever that boyfriend of hers is has fuckin connections because I just received a text from Cap to meet him at five in his office about the damn case. So whatever yo crooked ass promised him you better tell him you can deliver cause I am not going down with you." Detective Hunter lays out the evidence and what my lawyer put into motion after our call.

"Look you better get in line and fast otherwise your career will be the least of your worries." Perkins threatens him then walks off in the other direction. I lean my head against the while thinking about what I may have to do next if this corrupt as detective actually takes out his own partner before they can arrest the Judge. I shrug my shoulders at the thought though because it will always be whatever is necessary to protect my family. When I make it back to the room Arlani is back and arguing with some nurse.

"I met my nurse earlier and you sure as hell wasn't it.

"Hey, what's going on?" I shout walking in the room to see the nurse trying to put something in Arlani's IV, but she keeps moving away from the nurse and weakly pushing her back. When the nurse looks back at me she bolts out the room before I can turn to snatch her ass up but she drops the needle she was just trying to use. I take a picture of it then rush out the room to call out to detective Hunter who is standing near the nurses' station with the csi techs. They come back in to collect the evidence take some pictures, ask her about the nurse, and leave with hospital security to check the security video. I check on my baby and make them change her room asap. I'm trying to stay on the right side for her sake, but this bitch ass nigga is trying to keep me on my dark side.

Chapter Fifteen

Arlani James

It's been a week since that asshole kidnapped me then sent someone to kill me at the hospital. I haven't been back to the clinic as of yet not that I am scared but this concussion the cat scan confirmed I have has been keeping me in bed. It's been one dizzy spell or head after another. Kai is wonderful per usual either bathing with me or standing nearby as I do and the same with cooking. I can tell then he wants to take over, but he knows how important it is for me to get up and get around some, so he either hovers or helps. Today the detective is coming by with an update about the case since he doesn't want me to leave the house hell I don't quite want to either unless he's close by. Darren just left with Zion for school. He's been bringing him by this week after school even though it's his week because he knows I love my baby hugs when I'm not feeling good. I decide to lay on the couch until I hear the doorbell ring and Kai comes out of my office to answer the door.

"You feeling ok baby?" He kisses the top of my head and rubs my cheek.

"I'm ok babe just a mild headache. Go get the door before that prick breaks the doorbell." I joke sitting up fully and Kai just laughs as he struts off to the door. I swear every time I look at my man I want to jump his bones and it's not helping he went to get his locs retwisted and fresh line-up. Did I mention that elephant trunk of his showing through those damn basketball shorts and wells moisturized muscular arms and chest on full display since he has no shirt on.

"Detective Hunter, umph where's your partner?" He greets him and I notice once he steps in too that detective Perkins is not with him.

"He's no longer on the case." He answers as they walk over to where I am sitting on the couch. Detective Hunter sits on the armchair across from us.

"Well Detective what's the update you have for us?" Kai questions him getting right to the point.

"Well, the woman that came into your room Ms. James turned out to be a real nurse just not yours. I need you to look up a few photos and let me know if you recognize anyone." He pulls out a paper with pictures of a couple of women and I see the crazy ass woman that tried to jab me with a fuckin needle instantly, so I point to her.

"Ok that confirms our other evidence. We found her fingerprints on the needle that she dropped. It turns out the needle was just filled with air, which probably would've killed you if you in minutes were not up when she came in. I will have a warrant for her arrest within the hour. We are still trying to find out to whom the house you were held in belongs. The car was found burned to a crisp and we are still looking for the other man that took you. As far as the one that was shot he finally woke up a few days ago and for now is playing hard to get." I look up at Kai who has this blank look on his face, and I know that look my mans is about to act up.

"Well, that's all I have for you today. I will try to get more of an update for you next time and I hope you feel better Ms. James." He makes his exit, and I turn to Kai the moment he sits back down then wraps his arm around me.

"Kai don't even think about it. You better let them handle it." I warn him and he looks down at me with a smirk on his face.

"I won't but it's sad that I know that the shell company that owns the house is owned by the Judges wife's family. Either they're incompetent or they know and are hiding it. I will make it known to them since they are so fuckin slow but if they fumble the ball again I am handling shit myself my angel. There's not a chance in hell they are coming for you, and they better not even think about coming for Zion I will burn everything they love and make em watch." I think this man's crazy is starting to rub off on me because that shit just turned me on further than I already was. I turn and position myself on his lap facing him while I massage his dick through his shorts.

"Babe." He says in a warning tone that just incites a smile on my face.

"Protect me later fuck me till I'm crying your name out now." I entice him more by winding my hips over his growing dick.

"You better tell me if you feel the least bit dizzy or your head starts to hurt too much. I'm not joking Arlani getting my dick wet is not more important than your healthy." I nod my compliance, but I should've known that wouldn't fly. He pops my thigh his hand is resting on under my moo moo.

"Yes I understand babes." I answer him and he proceeds to do exactly what I wanted him too then carried me to bed to take a nap. I wake up to the smell of something good cooking in the kitchen. I swear that man's list of good traits is longer than my leg and being a curvy woman that stands at five feet eight inches that says a lot. The next few days are pretty much the calm, Kai did what he promised and turned in evidence to the police that Nas found the day before yesterday, but we haven't heard anything as of yet. I'm still not up to going back to the clinic so I am hanging out with Mymy at MoodHaus today while Kai checks on the gym and has a few clients. I'm not even sure how he gets anything done with the amount of text he's sent since dropping me off at eight this morning.

"Girl is my brother-in-law still blowing you up?" Mymy comes up to where I am standing dusting off some of the furniture up front since it's a little slow right now.

"Yes girl." I giggle.

"That man truly loves him some you and to think you almost didn't DM him." She teases me and I can't help but smile.

"See there goes that smile. We are living in some serious chaos right now, but you can still smile and it's any time you think about him. I'm really happy for you sis." We share a hug, and I ponder on her words until the door chimes. I turn to greet whoever has come in but stop dead in my tracks when my eyes meet with the Judge and what looks like a bodyguard. I hear a gun cock next to me, and I turn to see Mymy has pulled out a gun.

"If you want to keep that pretty face of yours Judge you will take you Igor looking bodyguard out the same door you came in." She threatens him with the gun aimed at his head. His confidence wanes for a moment when he realizes she's serious, but his cockiness returns quickly.

"Look I'm here for a truce since my wife is threatening to leave me and I can't have that so drop all the charges. In return I will leave you and your lil family alone. So, what do you say?" He stands tall, shoulders relaxed but back rim rod straight with his hands clasped together in front of him. I mean if he wasn't such a narcissistic shit head he would definitely be one of those salt and pepper zaddy's you I fucked from those social media videos, but he's killed that fuckin image.

"I'm not dropping shit, and you better listen to my sis here and walk back out the same door you came in." I respond pointing at the door with one hand and the other on my hip.

"Humph for a doctor you don't have much sense, but I guess you can take the girl out the hood, but you can't take it out of her. Last chance to accept my offer or I will tear your life apart and for fun I just may start with this little shop. You don't know who you are messing with little girl." This smug bastard has the audacity to threaten me again and Mymy doesn't take to kind to it. She sends off a shot that just barely misses his ear due to her not aiming at his head and his guard pulling him behind him. The guard draws his weapon, but the judge stops him.

"I told you to get the fuck out of my shop. The next time I shoot it will be right between the eyes." The moment she finishes her sentence the Kai comes in the front door and Nasir walks up behind us both with their guns drawn.

"You heard the lady leave before I break my promise to woman and drop yo ass where you stand."

Kai says coming around to the Judges side with his gun pointed at his head.

"Remember I tried to settle this amicably." He warns as he fixes his tailored suit jacket and taps his guard on the shoulder then starts heading for the door.

"You alright baby? I knew I shouldn't have left you." He rambles as he's checking to make sure they left then locks the door and turns the closed sign around.

"Babe I am fine you can't protect me twenty-four seven."

"Besides I had her sir relax." Mymy chimes in putting her gun back under her shirt.

"That's my girl." Nas praises her as he wraps his arms around her then kisses her all over the face making her break out into a fit of giggles. I can't help but smile at how cute those two are even though I'm becoming mildly annoyed at Kai and pissed the balls on this judge.

"Wait how did you guys know we needed you anyways?" I ask as Kai comes and wraps me up in his arms. I inhale his scent and instantly become at peace with my head rested on his chest as he squeezes me tight.

"Girl Nas has control of every camera and sensor in this place. Crazy ass even has a fifty-five-inch tv in company office and home office that plays the video to each one constantly."

"Yup I have a separate phone just that I check the video footage on while I'm too." He says like it's normal and I just shake my head because at this point why am I even surprised.

"But still doesn't explain how y'all got here so quick." I say after thinking about it for a second.

"We were on our way here to take y'all out to lunch." As soon as he says the word lunch my stomach growls and we all break out laughing. I call the detective on my case and Mymy sends him the video footage with sound apparently then we head out for lunch then to Zion's soccer practice. Once again with all the drama going on Kai finds a way to make me smile when he goes to stand by Darren and they fist bump each other then he leans down to give Zion a tight hug when he runs to him. I lean my head on Mymy's shoulder since she's sitting next to me and Nas has went down to stand with the guys.

Chapter Sixteen

Kairo Levi

"So that prick really pulled up to Mymy's boutique on some truce but then threatens her?" Darren says with his hands in his pockets rocking back and forth on his heels.

"Yea she called that sorry ass detective and had Mymy send him the info but he's not doing shit quick enough for me." I reply looking at our little did swing the bat then take off running.

"Look I know I am not as tough as you guys, but I've been taking gun safety lessons lately and actually bought one yesterday cause this shit is getting out of hand. I mean seriously what if he comes after Zion next and the guards aren't around? Hell, I feel crazy even having them around." He lets out a heavy sigh and we both place I hand on his shoulder.

"I know you have and keep them up but trust we are doing everything we can to make sure everyone is safe. I promised her I would let the police handle things first and if they don't do anything then we step in."

"Wait how did you know? I haven't even told Arlani yet."

"I make it my business to know everything about anyone that's going to be around my woman and my stepson. I'm pissed I found out about Farah's crazy ass too late." I inform him and chuckle at the stunned look on his face.

"You really love Arlani don't you and my son?"

"I did for them both, but I'd rather live to see the smiles on their faces every day." I confess. We had a heart to heart back when Zion was hurt but I didn't really express how I felt about them both.

"You know I had my reservations at first because of my stupid feelings but you are truly the right man for her and I'm glad we can all be cool and raise Zion together. The boy forever bragging about him having two cool dads." He laughs then claps as Zion slides across home plate and his coach signals for them to bring it in for the end of practice.

"Hey our parents and other siblings are in town for our family dinner night you and Zion are invited to come." I offer as we all make it back to the parking lot.

"Yea sure I can bring him by just send me the address." He replies.

"Dude he said you too. If he invites you to be around our family just accept the invitation cause he won't do it again and ya lucky he did in the first place." Nas says with a sigh then continues his walk to his truck opening the door for the ladies to get in.

"Ok we will both be there." He finally agrees so we fist bump, and I walk off to hop in the backseat with my soon to be wife. Lani's phones starts ringing the moment we walk across the threshold.

"Yes detective." She answers by placing the call on speaker phone.

"Ms. James you will be happy to know that Judge Joeseph will be coming in for questioning tomorrow morning but understand without more concrete evidence we can't press charges just yet." He explains and I wonder why the hell he even bothered calling. I walk over to where she's standing by the island in my kitchen and press the end call button. She just shakes her head then walks off to our room undressing as she goes. I look over at Nas and Mymy, who are still standing in the living room, and I nod my head then follow right behind her. When I walk in our room her clothes down to her lace panties are in a trail leading to the open bathroom door and I can hear the shower running. I continue my walk there still undressing and smile when I hear my nineties r&b playlist coming from the bathroom speakers then the footsteps behind me. When I get in the bathroom Lani's standing under the rain shower head swaying her hips to the music. I step in the shower behind her running my hands over her wet curves slowly followed by kisses down her spine right to that dip above her fat round ass. I stand back up and smack her on both ass cheeks as I lean over to bit down on her shoulder.

"Mhmm babe." She moans. I wink at Mymy who's standing at the door with Nas biting on her bottom lip as she removes the last bit of her clothing. I spin Lani around and she nods her head, so I pick her up to pin her against the back shower wall. She wraps her legs around my neck, and I bury my entire face in her wet pussy. I proceed to slurp up every bit of her juices until I feel Mymy come up on my side and touches my arm. I slowly release Lani's clit then lower her down to the shower seat. Mymy kneels next to me kissing her inner thigh then gliding her tongue over her clit in a circular motion. I add my tongue next hers and with both flick our tongues over Lani's sensitive clit.

"Ooooh fuck." She screams as her thighs begin to quiver, and she tries to close her legs.

"Unt... unt down you close those legs." Nas says as he stands next to Mymy then leans over grabbing Lani by the neck. I slide my tongue in her entrance just as her pussy starts to pulse and her creamy juices slide out.

"Fuck you're my favorite treat baby." I groan into her pussy. Mymy slides her in tongue in her pussy over mines and we do a seductive dance against each other licking up every drop of her essences.

"Now that's some sexy shit, mhmm." Nas moans. I look up to see Lani holding his dick. I don't sweat it because after the first time we had a discussion and our limits were the same, no pussy or ass penetration but everything else is cool. I slide my tongue between her pussy lips up to her clit and slurp her clit in between my lips. I switch in between slurping on it, sucking, and flicking my tongue until she's a cumming shaky mess. I hear Nas grunt then as quickly as that nigga came on my damn shower wall he had Mymy snatched up off the floor, bent over the seat licking his shit off the wall as he enter her from the back.

"Oooh fuck daddy just like that." She moans as he slams into her hard. She lifts one of her legs onto the seat.

"Fuck that's my girl." He groans. I pick a delirious Lani up turning to sit in the same spot then lowering her down on my hard dick that's been waiting all fuckin day to go home. We both continue to fuck our women into crying cumming messes then clean them and ourselves up before Nas and Mymy head to their room to get dressed.

"Shit babe I'm hungry as hell but I'm almost too tired to go plus I don't want yo parents looking at me like some fast as woman cause I'm sure I have thoroughly fucked written all over my face and how I'm walking." She murmurs as she lays back on the bed while I clasp her sandals on her ankle kissing each one as I finish.

"Babe my parents have been married for fifty years I am sure they could careless about the look on your face or your walk especially seeing as they know you are going to be their daughter in law sooner rather than later." I reach for her hand once I stand up then pull her up from the bed.

"Wow fifty years! I thought my parents had been married a long time and don't think I didn't catch that sooner rather than later, comment sir. It's no rush babe but let's go." She tries to walk past me, but I stop her with my hands on her waist.

"Wait you don't want to me?" I ask as I hold the bottom of her chin to look up at me.

"Of course I do Kai. I wouldn't love anything more than to be Mrs. Levi but I don't want you to feel pressured to do it so soon." She answers me.

"Woman I knew I was marrying you the moment I laid eyes on you across the room at my charity event and trust I had an inkling about it from our first video chat. So, understand I don't feel pressured to do shit." I make sure to look her in the eyes when I tell her to make sure she really feels what I am saying. Hell, I've been carrying the damn ring around for the past month and that's only cause I got it custom made along with her wedding bands. She puts her head down blushing but I lift it again giving her a quick kiss and tap on her hip at the same time a knock comes on our bedroom door.

"Hey bro mom called and you know how she is about us being late." Nas says through the door then I hear him walk off.

"Let's go baby before Zion and Darren beat us there." She tip toes to give me another kiss than we all head out to my parents' home that's about twenty minutes away thankfully because if we were any later Mrs. Ann Levi would break her foot off in our asses quick.

"Well, there goes my boys." Our mom greets us the moment we walk into family room and wraps us both up in hugs and kisses.

"Evening mama." Nas and I say in unison once she lets us go.

"There go my other daughters. You too look very mhmm- very happy." She says tapping on her chin and the girls almost turn beet red when they realize what she means. Me and Nas can't help but laugh a bit as she wraps them up in hugs and kisses next.

"Girls nothing to be ashamed of. Trust it is worse reasons to be running late. Trust Nasai and I have had quite a bit of those times." She giggles as my dad walks in from the kitchen tapping moms on the ass then pulls her into him then gives her quick kiss. Nas and I just shake our heads because we are used to their antics at this point but the girls both swoon.

"What have we had quite a bit of baby. Hey boys and ladies. Oh, by the rosy color on their cheeks I know now." He chuckles as he turns to pull mama with him to the dining room and tells us dinner is done. We greet our sisters and our oldest husband then our nieces and nephews. Darren and Zion show up moments later. He is shocked at how welcoming my family is towards him but becomes relaxed and smiles when he notices how my parents along with my sisters greet Zion with hugs and kisses like he's always been apart of the family. Dinner is filled with laughter and just all-around good vibes.

"Hey y'all come talk with me outside. Darren that includes you too." Dad says walking towards the back porch doors with cigars in hand and we all fall him out the door including our brother-in-law.

"What's up Pops." I ask once we all get outside and close the door.

"I reached out to some of my old associates about this Judge you are dealing with and he's one of those white men ass kissers. Made his money that he didn't get from his wife over sentencing and sending to certain prisons or detention centers. No one has spoken up against him and not landed in prison or dead." He looks over to me and I catch his drift quickly.

"Dad I am on it."

"I know you are, but I just want to make sure you understand what you are up against. We protect our women and children at all costs you know that, and I can tell things are very different with you and Arlani. Nas make sure you have yo brothers back, Darren I know I'm not your father, but you are Zion's, and I consider that little boy my grandson so I'm talking to you too when I say this if y'all need me to come up out of retirement let me know. I have more than a few places to hide some bodies." He says with a stern look on his face point at each of us with his lit cigar between is fingers. We all nod our heads and puff on the cigars he gave us.

"Hell let me know I will gladly hit up some of my military contacts." Dom my brother-in-law adds, and I will be having a private conversation with him about those contacts later. We stay out there talking about for about an hour or two with dad and Dom getting to know Darren amongst other things. When we finally leave the ladies are exhausted and both fall asleep on the ride home.

"Bro I know you promised her, but we are going to need to kill buddy. I received an alert at dinner someone was trying to get into Zion's school records, but I blocked it." Nas tells me once we get the ladies in bed.

"I'm already putting something together, don't worry." I inform him. I saw that look in his eyes this afternoon, so I know he's not going to give up and I know

my woman is not going to drop those charges against
Farah delulu ass. I send a test in our group chat with our
cousins and my brother-in-law for a meet up soon.
Once I finish the shot we poured I slide into the bed
slow to make sure I don't wake my angel and I pull her
into to me the moment I get comfortable.

Chapter Seventeen

Arlani James

Last week dinner with Kai's parents is still on my mind as I sit in my office this morning. I spoke with his mom and sisters about what he's been saying about marrying me and I just couldn't shake that he has been engaged before so what makes him so sure this time. After talking with them though I got another side to his last relationship and clearly the engagement was not about feelings but what he thought they should be doing based off how long they had been together. Now I'm wondering when he's going to pop out with this ring because I know my man and he already has a darn ring or at least knows which one he is going to buy. A knock comes at my office door taking me from my running thoughts.

"Come in." I call out.

"Doctor James your next patient Mrs. Joseph is waiting for you in exam room four." My assistant informs me. I hesitate at first because of the last name but shake it off as it can possibly be anyone. After grabbing what I need from my desk I walk over to the exam room and knock on the door. When I hear come in I enter the room and immediately stop in my tracks.

"Please don't be frightened. I am not here to cause any trouble. If anything, I hope I can be of help to you." The Judges wife jumps up to assure me.

"I'm not afraid. I'm annoyed. How exactly can you help me when your family is the cause of all my problems?" I question her walking fully into the room and closing the door. I have no qualms about fucking her old ass up if I have to, even in my clinic.

"I completely understand your annoyance. I recently felt that plus disgust when looking at my daughter and husband. Oh, nothing like that. My husband tends to hide a lot of stuff from me especially anything to do with our daughter well she's never really been ours. Ugghhh she is a product of Jeans early transgressions with another woman who passed away giving birth to her. I couldn't have kids at least I thought so but whatever I overheard him on the phone with someone planning to get someone by the name Kairo and Darren arrested on drug charges to get them out the way to get to you, but the worse part was hearing Farah bragging to one of her friends about burning a rugrat and her father helped her get off. I am done being in the dark and acting as if I don't know what's going on around me. Take this briefcase it's filled with files from when he was a sitting Judge and some other files I found on Farah. I am taking my families money and disappearing for good, good luck." She drops a bomb on me then walks out of the exam room leaving me completely stunned.

Kai walks into my office a couple minutes later while I am looking through one of the files I pulled out.

"What the hell did she want and why didn't you call me woman?" He questions the moment he closes the door.

"First watch your tone sir but I knew you saw her on the cameras and would be here sooner or later. Besides this damn briefcase she gave me is filled with so much shit my mind is blown. I really don't understand how the hell he was able to get away with all this." I say exasperated at the sheer amount of illegal shit this man has done and to think this is only what she could grab scares me. Kai walks over to my side and picks up one of the other files laying on my desk.

"Shit all this looks like it's before it was required for everything to be scanned into the system. Well, I guess we won't have to kill his ass after all."

"Try not to sound so disappointed sir. I already text for the detective to meet with us tomorrow. I figured you'd want to go through these and make copies just in case he's not shit either." I say opening another file with an insane amount of trumped-up charges on this woman who's probably in her sixties now.

"Wait a damn minute please tell me this lady doesn't look like who I think she looks like." I push the folder in front of Kai, and he gets the same look I did just a minute ago.

"Wait I thought the Judges wife was her mom. There's no way this isn't her real mother."

"Oh, about that." I say and start telling him everything she told me. We pack up once we realize how late it is, and he has Nas meet us at my house to keep going through the files. It turns into a family affair because the moment everyone heard about the files they just had to see them for themselves. So, his cousins, Darren, and his brother-in-law came over and of course Mymy came with Nas. Kai makes some finger foods while I get cleaned up and by the time I come back downstairs the food is done and everyone is sitting in the living room. I take a seat on Kai's lap then fill everybody in on what the Judges wife told me.

"Wait so the crazy bitch is not even her daughter but his cheat baby that he moved into their home as an infant by lying that the woman was dead but in reality he put the broad on jail for life." Darren says completely flabbergasted at this man audacity.

"Pretty damn much. Oh, and you three until this shit is cleared don't drive by yourselves and if you get puller over get out the car with your hands up, refuse to have your car searched by locking them in the car. If they want to call a tow truck decline and call your own plus a damn lawyer. He plans on setting y'all up to be arrested on drug charges since that's what will keep y'all the longest." I tell them and Kai pinches my thigh because I left that out earlier.

"So, what's the plan because looking at these files I'm ready end his ass tonight." Juice states slamming the file closed he was reading through.

"Shit same. Jail is too good for his Uncle Tom ass." Goon his other cousin who I swear looks like the rapper 2 Chainz. The more we look at these files though and the other judges' names that are in them along with prosecutors I think this has gotten bigger than us.

"Look I hear y'all but y'all don't see these other names that are in these files. I see how he's been able to get away with so much for so long. Some of the old prosectors are sitting judges, this one is the attorney general, he's moved to become a mayor, and this shit gets worse. Killing him is not the answer."

"Ok so what do you think we should do then baby?" Kai says as he rubs my thigh.

"I think we need to make copies and release them to a news outlet for all the others but his I still want to give it to the detective tomorrow and let's see what he does with it. If he fumbles then y'all have at it. I just don't want any of you to end up like these men in these files." I look around at all the men in the room and it really settles in me how anyone of them could have been in these files spending the rest of their lives basically in a cage for some shit they didn't do. They all nod their understanding and for a moment the mood in the room becomes solemn, but Mymy changes it with a drinking game so by the end of the night we are all to drunk to move. Somehow Kai and I made it to my bed at least so when the loud knocking comes I'm at least not waking up with a hangover and crank in my neck. I notice Kai isn't in bed then I hear his voice downstairs answering the door for the detective. I make it to the bathroom and scare the shit out of myself with my hair all over my head, slob stuck to the side of my mouth, and crust all in my eyes. I quickly get my hygiene together and get myself presentable. When I make it out of the bathroom Kai is sitting on the edge of the bed.

"The Detective is waiting downstairs with my cousins looking like a scared mouse and Nas was able to scan all the files as well as make copies with Mymy help in your office. You ready?" He informs me and the only thing I am wondering is how in the hell were they up so early plus functional.

"So have you actual done any work on her case or have you just relied on my cousins?" I hear Juice questioning the detective quite aggressively when we reach the top of the stairs.

"Juice." I call his name sternly. He looks up at me with a smirk then leans back in his with his arms crossed on his large chest. I see why detective Hunter looks so intimidated I forgot how big all these men are. Like the shortest one is probably six foot one since Darren isn't here.

"Ms. James you needed to speak with me." Detective Hunter stands and walks towards me.

"Yes. I was given some information about the Judge you need to finally arrest him." I hand him the file Kai gave back to me upstairs. He takes the file and flips through getting the same look I had when looking over it.

"Before you even think about pushing this under the rug we have copies of that file and will gladly release them ourselves then include you." Kai warns him.

"I wouldn't even think about it. The reason things have been moving a little bit slowly is because of the internal investigation into my partner you met the first day. We had a conversation that I recorded and had submitted as evidence to prove he's corrupt." My mind is once again blown. Kai told me about the conversation he overheard but thought nothing ever became of it.

"This is just what I need to bring them all down. I promise I will get them arrested by the end of day."

"Hey, you seem like one of the good ones so watch ya back brother. It's a lot of names in that one file." Dom warns him as he leans on the back of the couch with his hands in his pockets. Once the detective leaves we figure things out then go our separate way. It's been a few days since the detective left, and the news has been going crazy with arrest. Kai and Nas hired security around the clock for the entire family. Tonight, we are meeting back up at his parents for some good family fun. This time everyone is there, even my parents and I really need this tonight with everything going on especially after getting that damn witness subpoena. When I walk outside to the backyard where we all are gathering my eyes fill with tears instantly. Kai is at the end of a long cream-colored runner with family on either side hold a red or white rose and they each hand it to me as I walk towards them. My mom hands me her handkerchief because I can barely see through my tears. I reach Kai he's standing in the middle of heart shaped candles.

"Arlani... I asked your dad, and I asked Zion too—he said I could have you if I still let him sleep in the bed sometimes." He smiles softly at him next to me, then he grows serious.

"I've loved you from afar, in silence, in strength, in every damn breath since the day you hearted that first DM. You've given me peace, purpose, a little dude to love and I've never felt more like a man than when I'm loving you. So, if you'll let me... I wanna love you loud for the rest of my life. Will you marry me, my angel?" He asks as he kneels, this beautiful colored floral arrangement that says "Will you marry me" lights up and opens the ring box Zion just handed him then goes back to standing next to my mom and dad. The ring is a beautiful teardrop shaped moonstone in the middle of two half crested moon on a thin gold band that has small diamonds in it. I thought I was crying before, but tears are literally sliding down cheeks in streams.

"Yes... Yes I will marry you." I finally answer. He slides the ring on my finger picking me up as he stands and spins be around as we connect our lips in a heated kiss that's filled with so much love I feel like my heart may burst.

"I love you so much." I whisper over his lips, and he says the same. When he finally puts me down the family engulfs us in hugs and congratulations. We drink, dance, and eat the rest of the night.

Chapter Eighteen

Kairo Levi

It's been about two weeks since I proposed to my angel, and I am glad I was able to give us both the peace we needed even if it was just for one night. The Judge was publicly indicted after trying to get off on the charges, Farah tried to run but with her dad's assets frozen and his wife formally writing her off she didn't get far or go for long. Those that could turn on him to get set free or at least reduced charges did so quick as hell. I just pulled into the back of Lani's clinic, and I dap up the security that I hired to always protect the place after there was an attempted break in earlier in the week.

"Hi fiancé you ready to go home?" I greet her once I enter her office to find her staring blankly at the tv, so I turn to see what she's staring at and it's a news alert about Farah being stabbed to death in jail by her biological mother who was apparently being held there to stand trial as a witness

"Well damn." That is all I can say once as I stand behind her chair and start rubbing her arms to bring her back to me.

"Oh, shit babe I didn't realize you were here."

"I know baby it's ok."

"Can you believe it though. Like she was killed by her own mother. They say she was screaming about her being the devil and never should have been born." She tells me what the news alert said as she finally comes out of her trance fully.

"That's fucked up bad, but we have other things to deal with. Farah had the day she deserved." I remind her as we must get to Zion's soccer game in about forty-five minutes.

"You right my babies first game is tonight." I move from behind her chair so she can push it back and stand for us to leave. We ride in silence but hand in hand and seeing my ring on her finger has my chest feeling all warm making my damn dick hard, but I will save that for later. She makes quick work of getting ready and we soon pull up to the soccer field right before the game starts. All the fam has showed up for him tonight down to my cousins, aunts, and of course my parents. We all take up the first eight rows of benches it's so many of us. When he turns around to wave at us his jaw drops when we all shout his name and show off our shirts with his name and number on them. We cheered all night even when it looked like they were going to lose and then baby boy makes the winning goal. I know they were pissed with us, but we rush the field cheering. Darren and I throw him up on our shoulders bouncing him up and down. We go out to dinner to celebrate with his team and take up the entire restaurant.

"Hey baby let me talk to you for a minute." I grab Arlani's hand to walk to the side of our group as everyone is getting ready to leave the restaurant, so we are all waiting on the valets to bring our cars.

"Everything ok babe?" She has concern written all over her face.

"It's nothing bad baby. I wanted you to myself when I show you this." I pull out our boarding tickets for the entire family to the Maldives and we leave the day after tomorrow since she has to testify. She starts going through the envelope and gets the biggest smile on her face. She gets so giddy she begins hopping on her tippy toes.

"Babe are you serious right now? These are a lot of tickets."

"Yea Nas and I put it together. We all need to get away and have some fun after the mess you will have to deal with tomorrow." Before she can respond a car tire screech and shots start ringing off in a rapid succession. I pull her behind me and search the thinned-out crowd to find our family but find my cousins and Nas guns in hand sending shots towards the car that started the shooting. It starts rolling slowly down the street then crashes into a parked car. I turn to Lani and examine every visible inch.

"I'm ok babe." She shouts trying to get around me, however I know who she's going for and I turn around myself to look for him. We find him being examined by both sets of grandparents who look fine as well. Nas and all eight cousins are checking out the driver of the car as police sirens start coming down the road. I breathe a sigh of relief that hurts too damn much for my liking. When I try to take the next one I can't. I start feeling woozy, so I try to lean against the car, but my hand slips and I fall with my hands outstretched to keep from face planting on the concrete.

"Babe. Kairoooo." Is the last thing I hear from my lady before everything goes dark. My only regret is that I didn't get to change my angel's last name to mine. I start feeling cold, but that pain is still constant and soon I don't feel that either. The saying that you see some bright white light at the end is bullshit.

The End

Epilogue

One Year Later – Arlani Levi

I can't believe it's been a year since the chaos ensued upon my damn life but brought in the love of my life and damn near took him from me in the same breath. Kai spent about a week in the hospital due to a collapsed lung, lacerated liver and two broken ribs because he was shot twice. The pain of seeing him sprawled out on the ground with blood seeping from his side covering my hands and the concrete under our feet. We decided to get married in his hospital room the day after he woke up. Nas crazy ass took the test online to be able to ordain our wedding. I wore a simple white dress, the moonstone gold jewelry set he bought with our matching titanium wedding bands but then he had a gold one made that has moonstones in the band. Right now, I'm laying on the beach chair soaking up all the sunrays the Maldives has to offer. Zion is playing in the crystal blue water with Darren and the rest of the family.

"How my angels doing?" Kai asks as he sits in the beach chair next to me then rubs my semi protruding belly since I am about four months pregnant. That man wasted no time putting a baby in me after I told him I had take out my birth control implant.

"We are good over here. Nice, warm, and full thank you very much Papi." I respond rubbing my feet together feeling so relaxed.

"You know what that does to me baby." He groans as he leans over and kisses my neck.

"Don't you start I am too damn full and comfortable to move sir." I push his butt away from me giggling.

"Stop you're going to make me pee on myself." I laugh harder as he keeps kissing my neck and exposed chest. I don't even know why I let him convince me to wear a damn two piece with this damn belly I'm carrying now.

"Fine but I'm getting in that later." He warns then gives me a kiss and goes to play with the fam in the water while I take me a much need nap. I am so happy I use to dream of having a large family with everyone healthy and happy and now I am living those dreams even if it was a rough road getting here. Now my dreams are filled with the face of our new baby but surprise for Kai is it's two babies, but I will tell his overprotective ass about that when we get home.

Kairo Levi

Splashing in the water with my little dude knowing the wife is laying nearby baking my two little ones is making this one-year anniversary of damn near leaving this world that much better. I'm not sure why after almost two years together she still thinks she can hide anything from me, but I will let her think I don't know. My mind just wrapped around the fact that I really almost lost everything in front of me because of the bitch ass judge. I smile anyways looking over at Nas and Mymy playing in the water with my nephew. Now that one surprised us all when she went into labor on our family trip to Miami a few months back. I never knew it was possible for a woman to go eight months and not know she's pregnant but according to mom's that shit happens. Those two got married a month back, Mymy was adamant she "snapback" as she calls it a little bit before putting on her wedding dress.

"Papa look... look what I found with daddy." Zion shouts as he runs through the water to me.

"These look cool Babyboy." I look at his shiny seashells in amazement.

"Papa are we still going to be this close when the new baby comes?" My pops told me that question would come soon enough.

"Of course we will. Now will Mom and I be a little busy at times because your new siblings will depend on us more, but I will always be your Papa, understand?" I explain to him taking the advice from my Pops and I see him nodding his approval across the way. We stay out in the water until the maid lets us know the dinner is done. While sitting next to the wife my phone chimes and I notice the look on Nas's face.

"Baby let me check on this I will be right back." I give her a kiss on the cheek then excuse myself from the table and so does Nas. We meet up in the office off the kitchen and I pull my phone back out to open the text message I received. The message is from one of Juice's boys back home with a video message, so I press play.

"So, Judge Joseph you like to play with people lives for that sorry pussy ass well dead ass daughter of yours." Some dude off to the side of the video taunts the judge with a shiv poking at his bare chest.

"Yea he does. Staking up charges on people that either do what he wanted or just so he can line up his pockets with his rich white friend's money. You see what that got your bitch ass." Another taunt.

"Yup it got you right here with us but not for long though. You messed with the wrong ones this go around." He says then shoves the blade into his side then multiple men come into frame doing the same repeatedly until his body goes limp. He has at least twenty stab wounds spread all over his mid-section and blood is pooling at his feet. The last person that comes into frame shocks the shit out of me because the judge is in an all-male prison and the woman standing in frame now clearly is not a guard but is dressed like one but not so well. When she turns slightly I recognize her as the judge's mistress. She testified a year ago about the judge being the man that sent her husband to prison and told her if she slept with him that he would let him off with probation but instead he tacked on more years. When she found out she was pregnant she made the mistake of telling him, so he kept her comfortable until she had the baby then had drugs planted on her along with a gun that was connected to the murder of a drug dealer. He sent that poor woman off to prison just a week after having their baby. After she testified her prison sentence was rescinded along with a lot of other folks. She stands in front of him for a minute then one of the guy's hands her a blade and she slices his stomach open right down the middle then spits on him and leaves then the video ends.

"Well damn that was definitely the best revenge. Well let's get back to our family that bitch ass nigga is gone for good. You have two on the way and my little dude is terrorizing his moms at the dinner table." Nas reminds me then pats me on the shoulder and turns to leave. He's right so I delete the video and walk back out to our family. I do tell my wife what happened, but I don't give her any details and thankfully she didn't ask either. I look over the extra-large dining table at all the family laughing and enjoying the good food and kiss Lani's hand then sit back in my seat with a smile that has been tattooed on my face since the moment she replied to my DM. I guess you can find love on social media.

About The Author

Hey y'all thank you for once again reading one of my creations! If you are new here I'm Lala B., a 35-year-old mama of two and a recent country girl transplant. I've been writing for pleasure since I was a kid, and in February 2025, I finally published my first book—dream come true! With a background in tech and a wild imagination, I pour my heart into every page. I love thrillers, romantasy, dark romance, urban romance, and sooo much more. If it's bold, emotional, and a little messy—I'm all in. Welcome to my world!

Purchase your books at www.sipngrabyouabook.com

Find Me On Social Media:

Facebook- https://facebook.com/authorlalab

Facebook Group:
https://www.facebook.com/share/g/15GNVHNitN/

Tiktok: https://tiktok.com/authorlalab

Instagram: https://instagram.com/authorlalab

Amazon Profile:
https://www.amazon.com/author/authorlalab

Books By The Author

Love Unconventional: The Fredericks Family Series

Love Unapologetic: The Fredericks Family Series

I Married My Dead Cousin's Husband